SIMULACRON-3

SIMULACRON-3

DANIEL F. GALOUYE

ARC MANOR
ROCKVILLE, MARYLAND

SHAHID MAHMUD
PUBLISHER

www.CaezikSF.com

ISBN: 978-1-64710-030-8

First CAEZIK Notables Edition. 1st Printing. July 2021.
1 2 3 4 5 6 7 8 9 10

An imprint of Arc Manor LLC

www.CaezikSF.com

INTRODUCTION

✖INTRODUCTION✖
by Richard Chwedyk

RETURN WITH US NOW TO those thrilling days ….

Okay, so maybe you don't remember those thrilling days. So, imagine them with us.

It's 1964. Lyndon Johnson is in the White House. He's running for president against someone named Barry Goldwater. Young people are listening to new bands from England, when they're not demonstrating for civil and voting rights. The U.S. military is getting mired in a place called South Vietnam. The military takeover in Brazil. Harold Wilson. Jomo Kenyatta. Riots in Harlem. Riots in Singapore. *The Beverly Hillbillies*. All these names and places on the television and in the newspapers, but you pay little attention to them. You're young, and television is for watching *The Twilight Zone* or *The Outer Limits*, or if you pay attention to the news, it's to find out the latest report about the Mariner 3 space probe, launched from Cape Kennedy.

You're a science fiction fan.

And you walk into the local corner drugstore.

The drugstore is unaffiliated—not part of a chain—or if affiliated, it's with a chain like Rexall. The orange and blue sign above the door gives it away. Inside, the store is packed with everything, and has shelves up to the ceilings. Not only are there a million bottles behind the pharmacist's counter, but those packed shelves contain everything from throat lozenges to cotton gloves, to thermometers, to bedpans, to shampoo. They even have toys and displays of penny candy. The floor is wooden and creaks when you walk on it, even if you weigh only 88 pounds. The place has a smell, too: like molasses mixed with alcohol and cherry cordial. It smells like nothing you would ever willingly imbibe, but at the same time there's an assuring familiarity about it: you could close your eyes, inhale, and know instantly where you are. This little drugstore has no soda fountain, as many did, once upon a time, but that's no matter. It has something far more tempting—and irresistibly so—than ice-cream, chocolate syrup and phosphates.

It has a tall display shelf of comic books—loaded with everything from *Kona – Monarch of Monster Isle* to *Richie Rich's Millions*. And two shelves of magazines, including the latest monster magazines, *Mad*, and all the science fiction digests: *Analog, Galaxy, Fantasy and Science Fiction*, If, *Amazing Stories, Fantastic*.

And next to the magazine shelves are two spinner racks. And a third spinner rack across the aisle. And on those spinner racks—

Paperbacks!

In those days, marketing "experts" hadn't yet taken over (but keep them in mind, since we're coming back to them), and distributors were not yet amalgamated into a publishing version of the Borg. Those spinner racks carried a little of everything: westerns, romances, movie "novelizations," thrillers, mysteries—

Science Fiction!

And the science fiction books weren't all the same (though some of the covers made them appear so). It wasn't all Asimov, Heinlein and Clarke. And it wasn't all space adventure and invading aliens. And they weren't all written in the same way. Most of the bylines were male, but there was a diversity of styles and approaches—straight dramatic, satirical, pulp-ish, even (gasp!) literary—but who knew what that was when you were a kid and a science fiction fan? And all these names: Pohl, Sturgeon, Harrison, Simak, Sheckley, Silverberg, Brown, Tenn, Budrys, Dick, Norton, Bradley, Brackett, Brunner, Leiber, Pangborn, Matheson, Gunn, Vance, Anderson—who *were* these people?

Yet there they all were, spinning on the same spinner rack.

And spinning with them on that same spinner rack was Daniel F. Galouye.

Daniel *who?*

Not that it mattered. This rack was for discovering new names. Exploring new fictional universes. Who knew who the other authors were on that spinner rack?

The cover was eerily evocative. The planet Earth encased within a translucent rectangular prism. Lunar-like mountains in the background, and above them, stars. Along the bottom foreground, a row of anonymous human figures, not much more than silhouettes.

The title: *Simulacron-3*. What could it mean?

You read the first few paragraphs. Not deathless prose (but what do you know of deathless prose anyway? You're a science fiction kid) but it lays out a scene, gives you a place, introduces an intriguing situation. This might be a great read. Or it might be bore. It's not a long book. At worst, it could bore you for a couple of days.

You look up at the price: forty cents.

Even on your skimpy allowance, forty cents is a reasonable investment, a decent risk.

You take the book to the girl behind the cash register, a nice kid from Queen of Peace High School, still in her uniform. She rings up the purchase and looks you over. She might be a science fiction reader too. You never know. At least she's not the frumpy woman in harlequin glasses who always looks at you as if you're buying pornography.

The Queen of Peace girl slips your book and the receipt into a little paper bag and hands it to you. "This any good?"

"We'll find out," you say.

"Let me know if it is."

She's one of us, you think, though "us" may be no more than yourself and your cousin who lives two counties away (it's always been that way with science fiction fans). But you say, "Sure thing," and leave the hallowed, sacred confines of the local Rexall.

So, what will you find in *Simulacron-3*?

Authors of the caliber of Mike Resnick have noted an obvious proto-Cyberpunk connection. All you need are smaller computers, a *film noir* milieu upgraded to *Blade Runner* production values, mirror shades and leather jackets, and *voilà*—you can shelve this next to Gibson, Shirley, or Sterling. At this time (meaning 1964), Philip K. Dick had already been playing around with simulated realities, and Frederik Pohl's classic "The Tunnel Under the World" had already placed the mechanism of such replica realities in the hands of the advertising industry.

What has so far gone unremarked upon is Galouye's prescient focus on the importance of what in simpler times was called "market research": data mining, clickbait, the constant and relentless pursuit of finding out what "the rest of us" like, despise, purchase, endorse, or condemn. The people who are in the business of influencing us—to buy, to sell, to vote, to live—will stop at nothing to gather every scrap of information they can digitize in order "to serve you better."

And Galouye was already wise to this scam—er, to the fact that for all the stated benefits of their knowing your every nook and cranny of opinion and predilection produces not a greater variety of things, but a greater *uniformity*—a greater *sameness* of things. Because the benefactors of that great market that constitutes our present culture is not so much interested in giving you what you want to buy, but selling you what they want to sell you. And nothing more.

It is this aspect of Galouye's novel that speaks to us now, in this day, more insistently and directly than it ever has before: more than Cyberpunk, more than VR, more than all the other futuristic accoutrements we have become inured to in our science fiction, whether we are casual readers or hardcore devotees.

Galouye made that clear to curious readers, in 1964, in that little corner drugstore. He was tapping us on the shoulder and whispering, "You'd better pay attention to this."

In this year, half a century later, his voice, his insistence, is even louder. Not too many books on that spinner rack can make the same claim.

Try it now, for yourself.

And by the way, let that girl at the drugstore cash register know it is worth her time.

SIMULACRON-3

✖ ONE ✖

FROM THE OUTSET, IT WAS apparent that the evening's activities weren't going to detract a whit from Horace P. Siskin's reputation as an extraordinary host.

On the basis of the Tycho Tumbling Trio alone, he had already provided the year's most fascinating entertainment. But when he unveiled the first hypnostone from Mars' Syrtis Major region, it was clear he had planted his distinction upon a new pinnacle.

As for myself, the trio and the stone, though intriguing on their own merits, sank to the level of the commonplace before the party was over. For I speak with exclusive authority when I say there is nothing as bizarre as watching a man—just disappear.

Which, incidentally, was *not* part of the entertainment.

As commentary on Siskin's lavish excesses, I might point out that the Tycho Tumblers had to have lunar-equivalent gravity. The G-suppressor platform, bulky and anomalous in its lush setting, dominated one of the rooms of the penthouse suite while its generators cluttered the roof garden outside.

The hypnostone presentation was a full production in itself, complete with two doctors in attendance. Without any inkling of the incongruous developments the evening held in futurity, I watched the proceedings with detached interest.

There was a slim young brunette whose piercing, dark eyes clouded and rained tears freely as one of the stone's facets bathed her face with soft azure reflections.

Ever so slowly, the crystal rotated on its turntable, sending shafts of polychromatic light sweeping across the darkened room like the spokes of a great wheel. The radial movement stopped and a crimson beam fell upon the somewhat cautious face of one of Siskin's elderly business associates.

"No!" He reacted instantly. "I've never smoked in my life! I won't now!"

Laughter brimmed the room and the stone resumed rotation.

Perhaps concerned that I might be the next subject, I withdrew across plush carpeting to the refreshment alcove.

At the bar, I dialed the autotender for a Scotch-asteroid and stood staring through the window at the sparkling city below.

"Punch me a bourbon and water, will you, Doug?"

It was Siskin. In the subdued light he seemed inordinately small. Watching him approach, I marveled over the inconsistencies of appearance. Scarcely five feet three, he bore himself with the proud certainty of a giant—which indeed he was, financially speaking. A full head of hair, only slightly streaked with white, belied his sixty-four years, as did his almost unlined face and restless, gray eyes.

"One bourbon and water coming up," I confirmed dryly, dialing in the order.

He leaned back against the bar. "You don't seem to be enjoying the party," he observed, a suggestion of petulance in his voice.

But I let it go without recognition.

He propped a size five shoe on the rung of a stool. "This blowout cost plenty. And it's all for you. I should think you'd show *some* appreciation." He was only half joking.

His drink came up and I handed it over. "*All* for me?"

"Well, not entirely." He laughed. "I'll have to admit it has its promotional possibilities."

"So I gathered. I see the press and networks are well represented."

"You don't object, do you? Something like this can give Reactions, Inc., an appropriate send-off."

I lifted my drink from the delivery slot and gulped half of it. "REIN doesn't need a send-off. It'll stand on its own feet."

Siskin bristled slightly—as he usually does when he senses even token opposition. "Hall, I like you. I've got you pegged for a possibly

10

interesting future—not only in REIN, but perhaps also in some of my other enterprises. However—"

"I'm not interested in anything beyond Reactions."

"For the present, however," he continued firmly, "your contribution is singularly technical. You stick to your knitting as director and let my promotional specialists take care of their end of it."

We drank in silence.

Then he twisted the glass in his tiny hands. "Of course, I realize you might resent not holding any interest in the corporation."

"I'm not concerned with stock. I'm paid well enough. I just want to get the job done."

"You see, it was different with Hannon Fuller." Siskin stretched his fingers tensely around the glass. "He invented the hardware, the system. He came to me seeking financial backing. We formed the corporation—eight of us did, as a matter of fact. Under the arrangement, he came in for twenty per cent of the pot."

"Having been his assistant for five years, I'm aware of all that." I dialed the autotender for a refill.

"Then what *does* have you out here sulking?"

Reflections from the hypnostone crept across the ceiling of the alcove and splashed against the window, fighting back the brilliance of the city. A woman screamed until her shrill cries were finally subdued by a swell of laughter.

I pushed upright from the bar and stared insolently down at Siskin. "Fuller died only a week ago. I feel like a jackal—celebrating the fact that I'm stepping up into his job."

I turned to leave, but Siskin quickly said, "You were going to step up regardless. Fuller was on his way out as technical director. He wasn't standing up under pressure."

"That isn't the way I heard it. Fuller said he was determined to keep you from using the social environment simulator for political probability forecasts."

The hypnostone demonstration ended and the din that had until then been acoustically smothered began flowing toward the bar, carrying with it a gesticulating group of gowned women and their escorts.

A young blonde in the vanguard of the charge headed straight for me. Before I could move away, she had pinned my arm possessively against

11

her gold-brocaded bodice. Her eyes were exaggerated with wonderment and silver-tinted pageboy tresses gamboled against her bare shoulders.

"Mr. Hall, wasn't it simply amazing—that Martian hypnostone? Did you have anything to do with it? I suspect you did."

I glanced over at Siskin, who was just then moving unobtrusively away. Then I recognized the girl as one of his private secretaries. The maneuver became clear. She was still on the job. Only her duties now were extracurricular, conciliatory, and across the boundary lines of the Siskin Inner Establishment.

"No, I'm afraid that was all your boss's idea."

"Oh," she said, staring after him in admiration as he walked off. "What an ingenious, imaginative little man. Why, he's just a doll, isn't he? A dapper, cuddly, little doll!"

I tried to squirm away, but she had been well instructed.

"And your field, Mr. Hall, is stim—stimulative—?"

"Simulectronics."

"How fascinating! I understand that when you and Mr. Siskin get your machine—I may call it a machine, mayn't I?—"

"It's a total environment simulator. We've got the bugs out at last—third try. We call it Simulacron-3."

"—that when you get your stimulator working, there won't be any more need for the busybodies."

By busybodies she meant, of course, certified reaction monitors, or "pollsters," as they are more commonly called. I prefer the latter, since I never begrudge a man the chance to earn a living, even if it means an army of—well, busybodies, prying into the everyday habits and actions of the public.

"It's not our intention to put anybody out of work," I explained. "But when automation fully takes over in opinion sampling, some adjustments will have to be made in employment practices."

She squirmed warmly against my arm, leading me over to the window. "What *is* your intention, Mr. Hall? Tell me about your—simulator. And everybody calls me Dorothy."

"There's not much to tell."

"Oh, you're being modest. I'm sure there is."

If she was going to persist with the Siskin-inspired maneuver, there wasn't any reason why I shouldn't maneuver too—on a level somewhat above her head.

"Well you see, Miss Ford, we live in a complex society that prefers to take all the chance out of enterprise. Hence, more opinion-sampling organizations than you can shake a stick at. Before we market a product, we want to know who's going to buy it, how often, what they'll be willing to pay; which appeal will work best in the religious conversions; what chance Governor Stone has for re-election; which items are in demand; whether Aunt Bessie will prefer blue to pink in next season's fashions."

She interrupted with a tinkle of laughter. "Busybodies behind every bush."

I nodded. "Opinion samplers galore. Nuisances, of course. But they enjoy official status under the Reaction Monitors' Code."

"And Mr. Siskin's going to do away with all that—Mr. Siskin and you?"

"Thanks to Hannon J. Fuller, we've found a better way. We can electronically simulate a social environment. We can populate it with subjective analogs—reactional identity units. By manipulating the environment, by prodding the ID units, we can estimate behavior in hypothetical situations."

Her glittering smile wavered, gave way to an uncertain expression, then was back again in full flower. "I see," she said. But it was apparent she didn't. Which encouraged my tactic.

"The simulator is an electromathematical model of an average community. It permits long-range behavior forecasts. And those predictions are even more valid than the results you get when you send an army of pollsters—busybodies—snooping throughout the city."

She laughed weakly. "But of course. Why, I never dreamed—be a doll, will you, Doug? Get us a drink—anything."

Through some misdirected sense of obligation to the Siskin Establishment, I possibly would have gotten her the drink. But the bar was lined four deep and, while I hesitated, one of the young bucks in promotion homed eagerly in on target Dorothy.

Relieved, I wandered over to the buffet table. Nearby, Siskin, flanked by a columnist and a network representative, was holding forth on the soon-to-be-unveiled marvels of REIN's simulator.

He beamed effusively. "Actually, it's possible this new application of simulectronics—it's a secret process, you know—will have such an impact on our culture that the rest of the Siskin Establishment will have to take a back seat to Reactions, Inc."

The video man asked a question and Siskin's response was like a reflex. "Simulectronics is *primitive* compared to this thing. Computer-based probability forecasting is restricted to *one* line of stimulus-response investigation. REIN's total environment simulator—which we call Simulacron-3—on the other hand, will come up with the answer to *any* question concerning hypothetical reaction along the entire spectrum of human behavior."

He was, of course, parroting Fuller. But from Siskin's mouth the words were only vainglorious. Fuller, by contrast, had believed in his simulator as though it were a creed rather than a three-story building packed with complex circuitry.

I thought of Fuller and felt lonely and inadequate to the challenge of continuing in his directorial footsteps. He had been a dedicated superior, but a warm and considerate friend. All right—so he *was* eccentric. But that was only because his purpose was all-important. Simulacron-3 might have been only an investment as far as Siskin was concerned. But to Fuller it was an intriguing and promising doorway whose portals were soon to open on a new and better world.

His alliance with the Siskin Establishment had been a financial expedient. But he had always intended that while the simulator was raking in contractual revenue, it would also be fully exploring the unpredictable fields of social interaction and human relations as a means of suggesting a more orderly society, from the bottom up.

I drifted over toward the door and, from the corner of my eye, watched Siskin break away from the newsmen. He crossed the room swiftly and shielded the "open" stud with his hand.

"Not thinking of walking out on us, are you?"

Obviously, he was referring to the possibility of my leaving the party. But, then again, *was* he? It occurred to me that I was an indispensable resource. Oh, REIN would go on to eminent success without me. But if Siskin was going to get *full* return on his investment, I'd have to stay on to implement refinements Fuller had confided to me.

Just then the buzzer sounded and the door's one-way video screen sparkled with the image of a slim, neatly-dressed man whose left sleeve was pinched within a Certified Reaction Monitor armband.

Siskin's eyebrows elevated with delight. "A busybody, no less! We'll liven up the party." He pressed the stud.

The door swung open and the caller announced himself: "John Cromwell, CRM Number 1146-A2. I represent the Foster Opinion Sampling Foundation, under contract to the State House of Representatives Ways and Means Committee."

The man glanced beyond Siskin and took in the clusters of guests around the buffet table and the bar. He appeared impatient and apologetically uncomfortable.

"Good God, man!" Siskin protested, winking at me. "It's practically the middle of the night!"

"This is a Type A priority survey, ordered and supported by the legislative authority of the state. Are you Mr. Horace P. Siskin?"

"I am." Siskin folded his arms and appeared even more as Dorothy Ford had described him—a dapper little doll.

"Good." The other produced a pad of official forms and a pen. "I'm to poll your opinion on economic prospects over the next fiscal year as they'll affect state revenue."

"I won't answer any questions," Siskin said stubbornly.

Knowing what to expect, some of the guests had paused to watch. Their anticipatory laughter was audible above the hum of conversation.

The pollster frowned. "You must. You are an officially registered interrogatee, qualified in the businessman category."

If his approach appeared stilted, it was. That's because reaction monitors usually rise to the occasion whenever their sampling contracts serve the public interest. Ordinary commercial polling procedures are not nearly as formal.

"I still won't answer," Siskin reiterated. "If you'll refer to Article 326 of the RM Code—"

"I'll find that recreational activities are not to be interrupted for monitoring purposes." The other cited his regulation. "But the privilege clause is inapplicable when sampling is in the interest of public agencies."

Siskin laughed at the man's obstinate formality, seized his arm and drew him across the room. "Come on. We'll have a drink. Then maybe I'll decide to answer after all."

Its "admit" circuit relieved of the pollster's biocapacitance, the door started to swing closed. But it paused and remained ajar in deference to a second caller.

Bald, lean-faced, he stood there scanning the room while his fingers meshed restlessly. He hadn't yet seen me because I was behind the door watching him through the video panel.

I stepped into view and he started.

"Lynch!" I exclaimed. "Where have you been for the past week?"

Morton Lynch was in charge of internal security at REIN. Lately, he had worked an evening shift and had become quite close to Hannon Fuller, who had also preferred night work.

"Hall!" he whispered hoarsely, his eyes boring into mine. "I've got to talk with you! God, I've got to talk with *somebody*!"

I let him in. Twice before, he had turned up missing—only to return haggard and wrung-out following a week-long electronic brain-stimulation binge. Over the past few days, there had been speculation over whether his absence had been a bereaved reaction to Fuller's death, or whether he had merely holed up in some ESB den. Oh, he was no addict. And even now it was plain he had not been on a cortical-current spree.

I led him out into the deserted roof garden. "Is it about Fuller's accident?"

"Oh, God yes!" he sobbed, dropping into a latticework chair and pressing his face into his hands. "Only, it *wasn't* an accident!"

"Then who killed him? How—"

"Nobody."

"But—"

To the south, beyond the scintillating lights that spread out like a carpet of symmetrical radiance far below, the Lunar Rocket loosed a thunderous roar and limned the city with crimson reflections as it lumbered spaceward.

As the sound erupted, Lynch almost bolted from his chair. I seized his shoulders and steadied him reassuringly. "Wait here. I'll get you a drink."

When I returned with the straight bourbon, he downed it in a single toss and let the glass drop from his hand.

"No," he resumed, no less shakily. "Fuller wasn't murdered. 'Murder' couldn't begin to describe what happened."

16

"He walked into a high tension lead," I reminded. "It was late at night. He was exhausted. Did you see it?"

"No. Three hours before then he and I had a talk. I thought he was crazy—what he told me. He said he didn't want to let me in on it, but he had to tell *somebody*. You were still on leave. Then—then—"

"Yes?"

"Then he said he thought he was going to be killed because he had made up his mind not to keep it a secret any longer."

"Not to keep *what* a secret?"

But Lynch was too wound up to be interrupted. "And he said if he turned up missing or dead, I would know it wasn't an accident."

"What was this secret?"

"But I couldn't tell anybody—not even you. Because if what he said was true—well, I guess I just spent the last week running and trying to decide what to do."

Held back until then by closed doors, the cacophony of the party surged out into the garden.

"Oh, *there* you are, Doug, darling!"

I *glanced* over at Dorothy Ford, silhouetted in the doorway and swaying against the effect of too many drinks. I emphasize the word "glanced" as a means of pointing out that my eyes could not have been off Morton Lynch for more than a tenth of a second.

But when I looked back at the chair it was empty.

17

✕ TWO ✕

By NOON THE NEXT DAY, Siskin's promotional efforts were reaping dividends. As far as I could ascertain, two morning video programs had presented "inside" commentary on the imminent development in simulectronics. And the early editions of all three afternoon newspapers carried front-page articles on Reactions, Inc., and its "incredible" total environment simulator, Simulacron-3.

In only one spot, however, could I find anything on Morton Lynch's disappearance. Stan Walters, in the *Evening Press*, had ended his column with this item:

> And it seems police are today concerned, but only superficially, with the reported "disappearance" of one Morton Lynch, supervisor of internal security at tycoon Horace P. Siskin's fabulous new property, Reactions, Inc. It would be our bet, however, that not much sleep is going to be lost in the search. The complainant claims that Lynch just "vanished!" It all supposedly happened at Siskin's penthouse party last night. And everybody knows that much more incredible things than that have been reported at Siskin blowouts.

Of course I had gone to police headquarters with the account. What else could I do? Watching a man disappear isn't something you simply shrug off and forget.

The intercom buzzer sounded on my desk but I ignored it, watching instead an air van lower itself onto the street's central landing island. Establishing its six-inch hovering altitude, the vehicle skewed across traffic lanes until it came to rest against the curb. A dozen men with

18

CRM armbands piled out.

Spacing themselves at intervals on the sidewalk in front of the REIN building, they hoisted placards that read:

SISKIN ESTABLISHMENT
THREATENS
MASS UNEMPLOYMENT!
SOCIAL UPHEAVAL!
ECONOMIC CHAOS!
—*ASSOCIATION OF REACTION MONITORS*

There it was—the initial, impulsive response to the labor-saving promise of simulectronics in its most advanced application. It wasn't new. The world had gone through such pangs before—during the Industrial Revolution, the Automation Transition.

The buzzer rang more insistently and I flicked the switch. Miss Boykins' face flared on the screen, anxious and impatient. "Mr. *Siskin* is here!"

Appropriately impressed with the visit, I urged the receptionist to send him on in.

But he wasn't alone. That much I could see via the screen. In the background, beyond Miss Boykins' image, were Lieutenant McBain of Missing Persons and Captain Farnstock of Homicide. They had both been in once that morning already.

Radiating indignation, Siskin burst into the office. His hands were drawn up into insignificant fists as he strode forward.

He bent over my desk. "What the hell are you trying to do, Hall? What's all this about Lynch and Fuller?"

I rose respectfully. "I merely told the police what happened."

"Well, it's stupid and you're making yourself and the whole Establishment look ridiculous!"

He came around the desk and I had to offer him my chair. "Nevertheless," I insisted, "that's the way it was."

McBain shrugged. "You're the only one who seems to think so."

I squinted at the plain-clothes man. "What do you mean?"

"I've had my department checking with every guest at the party. Nobody else even *saw* Lynch there last night."

Siskin lowered himself into the chair and his small form was swallowed within its curving arms. "Of course not. We'll find Lynch, all right—after we raid enough ESB dens."

He turned to McBain. "The guy's a cortical-current addict. This isn't the first time he's been out for his electrode kicks."

McBain stared severely at me, but addressed Siskin. "You sure *Lynch* is the one who's addicted?"

"Hall is all right," Siskin said grudgingly, "or I wouldn't have him in my Establishment. Perhaps he had a few too many last night."

"I wasn't drunk," I protested.

Farnstock moved in front of me. "Homicide's interested in what this fellow Lynch supposedly said about Fuller being murdered."

"He made it clear Fuller was not murdered," I reminded.

The captain hesitated. "I'd like to see where this accident happened and talk with someone who was there."

"It was in the function integrating room. I was on leave of absence at the time."

"Where?"

"At a cabin I have up in the hills."

"Anybody with you?"

"No."

"How about a look at that function room?"

"That's in Whitney's department," Siskin said. "He's Mr. Hall's assistant." He flicked a switch on the intercom.

The screen lit up, danced through a herringbone pattern or two, then steadied with the picture of a compact young man, about my age but with black, curly hair.

"Yes, Mr. Siskin?" Chuck Whitney asked, surprised.

"A Lieutenant McBain and Captain Farnstock will be coming down the hall in about ten seconds. Pick them up and show them through the function integrating department."

After the police officers had left, Siskin repeated himself. "What in the hell are you trying to do, Doug—wreck REIN before it even gets off the ground? In another month we'll start advertising for commercial research contracts. Something like this could set us on our heels! What makes you think Fuller's death wasn't an accident?"

"*I* didn't say it wasn't an accident."

He missed the distinction. "Anyway, who'd want to kill Fuller?"

"Anybody who doesn't want to see Reactions succeed."

"Like who?"

I jerked a thumb toward the window. "Them." It wasn't a serious indictment. I was just proving the point that felony was not all that far-fetched.

He looked and saw—for the first time, obviously—the Association of Reaction Monitors pickets. That brought him up out of the chair and sent him reeling into an elfinlike hop.

"They're *picketing*, Doug! Just like I expected! This'll put us squarely in the public eye!"

"They're worried about what REIN will mean to them—in terms of unemployment," I pointed out.

"Well, I just hope their apprehension isn't misplaced. Unemployment among the pollsters' association will be directly proportional to REIN's success."

He rushed out with an impulsive "See you later."

And he had left not a moment too soon. The room spun crazily and I staggered against the desk. I managed to lower myself into the chair, then my head slumped forward.

A few moments later I was all right again—uncertain and apprehensive, perhaps, but at least in possession of myself.

Then I realized I couldn't ignore my lapses of consciousness much longer. They were a good deal more frequent now. And even a month of rusticating at the cabin had done nothing to interrupt the pattern of sporadic seizures.

Nevertheless, I *wouldn't* give in to them. I was determined to see Reactions properly launched.

Nothing could convince me that Lynch hadn't actually disappeared. It *was* possible that no one else at the party had noticed his arrival. But that I had only fancied the entire incident was a concession I couldn't bring myself to make.

With that as a stepping-off point, three immediate incongruities had to be faced: that Lynch had, indeed, just vanished; that Fuller had, after all, not died accidentally; that there was some sort of "secret," as Lynch had put it, which supposedly had cost Fuller his life and resulted in Lynch's disappearance.

If I was going to verify any of those assumptions, however, it would have to be on my own. Police reaction had been about as unsympathetic as could be expected on so grotesque a complaint.

But it wasn't until the next morning that the only logical course suggested itself. That approach had to do with the system of communication that had existed between Fuller and me. It was also inspired by something Lynch had said.

Hannon Fuller and I had followed the practice of going through each other's notes periodically in order to co-ordinate our efforts. In making such memoranda, we used red ink to signify material that should be noted by the other.

Fuller, according to Lynch, had confided something of a secret nature to him. But the intimation was that I would have been told instead—if only I had been available. So it was just possible that Fuller had *already* arranged for transmission of the pertinent information—through the medium of red-ink notes.

I pressed the intercom switch. "Miss Boykins, have Dr. Fuller's personal effects been removed yet?"

"No, sir. But they'll have to be shortly. The carpenters and electricians are just about to descend on his office."

I remembered now: The space was going to be converted for other use. "Tell them to hold off until tomorrow."

When I found the door to Fuller's office ajar, I wasn't at all surprised, since we had been using his outer reception room to store simulectronic equipment. But after crossing the thick carpeting to the inner doorway, I drew back tensely.

There was a woman seated at the desk, thumbing through a stack of papers. That she had done a good rifling job was suggested by the still-open drawers and piles of articles beside the blotter.

I stole into the room, circling behind her and trying to draw as close as possible without being detected.

She was young, certainly not more than in her early twenties. Her cheeks, though rigid in the attention she was giving Fuller's papers, were smooth, evenly textured. Lips vied with rather large eyes as the dominant features of her face. The former, though full and vivid, had been rouged with a tasteful restraint. Intent upon the memoranda, her hazel eyes contrasted with ebon hair that flared out from a hat only token in size and somewhat impertinent in design.

I drew up behind her but delayed betraying my presence. Either she was here as an agent of one of the computer-type simulectronic foundations that stood to be pushed into the background by Reactions, or she was connected in some way with Fuller's cryptic "secret."

The girl had gone almost completely through the notes. I watched her turn over the second-to-last page and place it face down on the pile she had already inspected. Then my eyes fell on the final sheet.

It was in red ink! But there were neither words nor formulas nor schematic diagrams on it. Only a crude, meaningless drawing. The sketch showed a warrior of some sort—Grecian, judging from the tunic, sword and helmet—and a turtle. Nothing else. Except that each figure was heavily underlined with red strokes.

I might note here that whenever Fuller wanted to call my attention to something important in his memoranda, he underscored it one or more times, depending upon its significance. For instance, when he had finally drafted his transduction formula for programing emotional characteristics into the simulator's subjective reactional units, he had underlined it five times in heavy, red ink. As well he might have, since it was the cornerstone on which his entire total environment system was built.

In this case he had underscored the Grecian warrior and turtle at least *fifty times*—until he had run out of paper!

Finally sensing my presence, the girl sprang up. Fearing she would bolt for the door, I seized her wrist.

"What are you doing here?" I demanded.

She winced from the pressure of my grip. But, oddly, there was neither surprise nor fear on her face. Instead, her eyes were animate with a quiet, dignified fury.

"You are hurting me," she said icily.

For a moment I puzzled over the impression that I might have encountered those determined eyes, that diminutive, upturned nose before. I relaxed my grip, but did not release her.

"Thank you, Mr. Hall." There was no lessening of her indignation. "You are Mr. Hall, aren't you?"

"That's right. Why are you plundering this office?"

"Well, at least you're *not* the Douglas Hall I used to know." With an uncompromising pull, she freed her wrist. "And I'm *not* plundering. I was escorted here by one of your guards."

I stepped back, astonished. "You're not—?"

Her features remained frozen. And the very absence of moderation in her expression was affirmation enough.

Suddenly I was staring through her—past the proud image that blended a lingering demureness with newly-won sophistication—back through the haze of eight years to an awkward, fifteen-year-old "Jinx" Fuller. And I recalled that even then she had been pert and impulsive, surrendering none of her competence to dental braces, academy-style braids, and adolescent uniforms.

I even remembered some of the details: Fuller's embarrassment on explaining that his impressionable daughter had developed a "crush" on her "Uncle" Doug; the mixed emotions I felt from the lofty heights of twenty-five years' maturity and a soon-to-be-acquired Master of Science degree as Dr. Fuller's protégé graduate. Realizing how complicated fatherhood could be for a widower, Fuller had bundled his daughter off to a sister in another city for pseudomaternal upbringing and subsequent schooling.

She retrieved me from the past. "I'm Joan Fuller."

"Jinx!" I exclaimed.

Her eyes moistened and some of her self-assurance seemed to drain away. "I didn't think anybody would ever call me that again."

I took her hand solicitously. Then, purposely redirecting her attention, I explained my rudeness. "I didn't recognize you."

"Of course you didn't. And about my being here—I was asked to come pick up Dad's effects."

I led her back to the chair and leaned against the desk. "I should have taken care of it. But I didn't realize—I thought you were away."

"I've been back for a month."

"You were staying with Dr. Fuller when—?"

She nodded and purposely glanced away from the items she had gathered together on the desk top.

I shouldn't have pushed headlong into the matter at that particular moment. But I wasn't going to pass up the opportunity.

"About your father—did he seem concerned or worried?"

She looked up sharply. "No, not that I noticed. Why?"

"It's just that—" I decided to lie in order to avoid distressing her. "We were working on something important. I'd been away. I'm interested in finding out whether he solved the problem."

"Did it have anything to do with—function control?"

I studied her closely. "No. Why do you ask?"

"Oh, I don't know. It's nothing."

"But there must have been some reason for the question."

She hesitated. "Well, he was a little moody about something, I suppose. Spent a lot of time in his study. And I saw a few reference books dealing with that subject on his desk."

I wondered what gave me the impression she was trying to conceal something. "If you don't mind, I'd like to drop around sometime and run through his notes. I may find what I'm looking for."

That, at least, was more tactful than telling her I thought her father had not died accidentally.

She produced a plastic bag and began stuffing it with Fuller's personal effects. "You may call whenever you like."

"There's one other thing. Do you know whether Morton Lynch was around to see your father recently?"

She frowned. "Who?"

"Morton Lynch—the only other 'uncle' you had."

She looked uncertainly at me. "I don't know any Morton Lynch."

I concealed my perplexity behind grim silence. Lynch had been a university fixture—a maintenance man. He had come with Dr. Fuller and me when Fuller had left teaching for private research. Moreover, he had *lived* with the Fullers for more than a decade, having decided to move closer to the REIN building only a couple of years ago.

"You don't *remember* Morton Lynch?" I revived well-implanted memories of the elderly man building doll houses for her, repairing toys, riding her on his shoulders for endless hours at a time.

"Never heard of him."

I let it go and thoughtfully riffled through the stack of notes on the desk. I stopped when I came to the sketch of the Grecian warrior, but didn't linger on it.

"Jinx, is there anything I can do to help?"

She smiled. And with the expression returned all the warmth and casualness of her fifteen-year-old enthusiasm. For a moment, I felt a sense of loss that the "crush" had come so early in her life.

"I'll be all right," she assured. "Dad left a little. And I intend to be a working woman—with my degree in opinion evaluation."

"You're going to be a certified reaction monitor?"

"Oh, no. Not the sampling end of it. *Evaluation.*"

There was something ironic in the fact that she had spent four years training for a profession that would be made obsolete by what her father had done during the same period.

But sympathy wasn't in order. I indicated as much when I said, "You'll do all right with your interest in Reactions."

"Dad's twenty per cent? Can't touch it. Oh, it's mine. But Siskin wrapped it up in a legal arrangement. He holds the proxy. The stocks and dividends stay in trust until I'm thirty."

A complete squeeze-out. And it didn't take much imagination to see the reason. Fuller had not been alone in his insistence that part of the Reactions effort be dedicated to research toward lifting the human spirit from its still too-primitive quagmire. He had had enough other votes behind him to have made an issue of it at any board meeting. But now, with Siskin voting Fuller's twenty per cent, it was a cinch that the simulator would be wasted on no unprofitable, idealistic undertakings.

She folded the plastic bag. "I'm sorry for having acted rude, Doug. But I had a chip on my shoulder. All I could think of after reading about Siskin's party was you gloating over the fact that you had stepped into Dad's shoes. But I should have realized it's not that way."

"Of course it isn't. Anyway, things aren't working out the way Dr. Fuller wanted. I don't care for the setup. I don't think I'll be around much longer than it takes to see that his simulator becomes a reality. His efforts deserve that much satisfaction, at least."

She smiled warmly, tucked the bag under her arm and motioned toward the now-disheveled stack of notes. One corner of the page containing the red-ink sketch was exposed and I had the sensation that the Grecian warrior was staring derisively at me.

"You'll want to go through those," she said, heading for the door. "I'll be expecting you at home."

After she had gone I returned eagerly to the desk and reached for the memoranda. But I only jerked my hand back.

The warrior was no longer peering out at me. I went hurriedly through the stack of notes. The sketch wasn't there.

Frantically, then carefully, I raced through the sheets again and again. I searched the drawers, looked under the blotter and combed the floor.

But the drawing was gone—as surely as though it had never been there.

✶THREE✶

SEVERAL DAYS PASSED BEFORE I could dig deeper into the Lynch-Fuller-Grecian warrior enigma. Not that my anxiety wasn't compelling. Rather, I was hard pressed with the necessity of whipping the environment simulator into final shape and integrating all its functions.

Siskin kept cracking his whip. He wanted the system ready for full demonstration within three weeks, despite the fact that there were still over a thousand subjective reaction circuits to be incorporated in the machine in order to bring its primary "population" up to ten thousand.

Since our simulation of a social system had to amount to one "community," complete in itself, thousands of master circuits had had to be endowed with items of physical background. These included such details as transportation, schools, houses, garden societies, pets, government organizations, commercial enterprises, parks, and all the other institutions necessary to any metropolitan area. Of course, it was all done simulectronically—impressions on tapes, biasing voltages on master grids, notations on storage drums.

The end result was the electromathematic analog of an "average" city nestled unsuspectingly in its counterfeit world. At first I found it impossible to believe that, within the miles of wiring, the myriad transducers and precision potentiometers, the countless thousands of transistors and function generators and data-acquisition systems—within all these components reposed one entire community, ready to respond to any reaction-seeking stimuli that might be programed into its input allocators.

27

It wasn't until I had plugged into one of the surveillance circuits and seen it all in operation that I was finally convinced.

Exhausted after that full day of activity, I relaxed with my feet propped up on the desk and wrenched my thoughts from the simulator.

There was only one other direction in which they could go—back to Morton Lynch and Hannon J. Fuller, a Grecian warrior, a crawling turtle, and a formerly pixielike teen-ager called Jinx, who had matured, seemingly overnight, into a rather attractive but obviously forgetful young woman.

I bent forward and selected a toggle on the intercom. The screen responded immediately with the image of a white-haired, florid-cheeked man whose face was lined with fatigue.

"Avery," I said, "I've got to talk to you."

"For God's sake—not now, son. I'm bushed. Can't it wait?"

Avery Collingsworth—there's a Ph.D. behind the name—reserved the privilege of calling me "son," even though he was on my staff. But I had no objections, since I had once trudged diligently to his classes in psychoelectronics. As a result of that association, he was now psychological consultant for Reactions, Inc.

"It doesn't have anything to do with REIN," I assured him.

He smiled. "In that case, I suppose I'm at your service. But I'm going to impose one condition. You'll have to meet me at Limpy's. After today's workout I need a—" he lowered his voice, "—smoke."

"At Limpy's in fifteen minutes," I agreed.

I'm no inveterate law-breaker. On the Thirty-third Amendment I entertain no firm persuasions. The temperance groups, I suppose, have their point. At least, the position that nicotine was harmful to the health of the individual and the morals of the nation had not been without its substantiating statistics.

But I don't think the Thirty-third will stick. It's as unpopular as the Eighteenth was over a century ago. And I see no reason why a fellow shouldn't have an occasional smoke, if he's careful not to blow it in the direction of the Save-Our-Lungs Vigilantes.

In arranging to meet Collingsworth at a smoke-easy within fifteen minutes, however, I hadn't taken the CRMs into consideration. Not that I had any difficulty with the pickets in front of the building. Oh, they were vocal enough when I walked out. And there were even a few threats. But Siskin had exercised his influence and had a police detail stationed there on a twenty-four-hour basis.

What *did* delay me was the army of opinion samplers who invariably select late afternoon for their maximum effort, when they can prey upon the hordes leaving the offices and downtown stores.

Limpy's is only a few blocks from Reactions. So I had taken the low-speed pedistrip, which made me a sitting duck for any pollster who might come along. And come along they did.

The first, coincidentally, wanted to know all about my reaction to the Thirty-third Amendment and whether I might have any objection to a smokeless, nicotineless cigarette.

Hardly had he left than an elderly woman came up, pad in hand, to solicit my opinion on fare increases on the McWorther Lunar tour. That I never expected to take such an excursion made no difference.

By the time she had finished, I had been carried three blocks past Limpy's and could only continue on another two blocks to the first transfer platform.

Another certified reaction monitor intercepted me on the way back. He politely rejected my request to be excused, standing unflinchingly on his RM Code rights. Impatiently, I told him I didn't think packaged Mars taro, a sample of which he practically forced down my throat, would meet any justifying degree of consumer demand.

There were occasions—and this was surely one of them—when I could look forward almost wistfully to the era in which simulectronics would sweep the streets clear of all the swarming CRMs.

Fifteen minutes later than the appointed time, I was recognized and passed through the curio shop that fronted for Limpy's smoke-easy.

Inside, I waited for my eyes to adjust to the blue-haze murkiness. The acrid, yet pleasant odor of burning tobacco hung in the air. Omniphonic sound warmly embraced the room as tapestried walls muffled the strains of a period song, "Smoke Gets in Your Eyes."

From the bar, I scanned the tables and booths. Avery Collingsworth hadn't arrived. And I conjured up a humorous, yet pathetic picture of him doing his best to fend off a pollster.

Limpy came hobbling along the catwalk behind the bar. He was a stocky, seemingly perpetually perturbed little man with a twitch in his left eyelid that compounded his caricatural appearance.

"Drink or smoke?" he asked.

"A little of each. Seen Dr. Collingsworth?"

"Not today. What'll it be?"

"Scotch-asteroid—double. Two cigarettes—mentholated."

The latter came first, neatly bundled in a clear, flip-top plastic case. I took one out, thumped it on the bar and brought it to my lips. Instantly, one of Limpy's assistants thrust a blazing, ornate lighter in front of my face.

The smoke burned going down, but I fought off the urge to cough. Another draft or two and I was past the hump that invariably betrays an infrequent smoker. Then came the pleasant giddiness, the sharp but satisfying assault on nostril and palate.

A moment later, my euphoria was helped along by the soothing taste of Scotch. I sipped appreciatively, glancing out over the almost filled room. The light was subdued, the smokers restrained in conversation, so that a droning susurrus commingled with the archaic music.

Another period song was flowing from the speakers—"Two Cigarettes in the Dark." And I found myself wondering how Jinx felt about the Thirty-third, how it would be to relax with her in a roof garden and watch the glow of a cigarette cast crimson highlights on the satin smoothness of her face.

For the hundredth time I assured myself that she could have had nothing to do with the disappearance of Fuller's cryptic drawing. I went over it clearly in my mind. I had *seen* the sketch while walking her to the door. When I had returned to the desk, it was gone.

But, if she *wasn't* somehow involved, then why had she denied knowing Morton Lynch?

I swallowed the rest of the Scotch, ordered another and smoked the cigarette awhile. How simple it would all be if I could only convince myself there *was* no Morton Lynch—had never been any! In that case, Fuller's death wouldn't be under suspicion and Jinx would have been on solid ground in denying she had known him. But, still, that wouldn't explain the missing drawing.

Someone climbed onto the stool next to mine and a stout, gentle hand descended on my shoulder. "Damned busybodies!"

I glanced up at Avery Collingsworth. "Got you too?"

"Four of them. One hit me with a Medical Association personal

30

habits survey. I'd rather have a tooth pulled."

Limpy brought over Collingsworth's pipe, its bowl filled with the house's special mixture, and took his order for a straight whiskey.

"Avery," I said thoughtfully while he lit up, "I'd like to toss you a picture puzzle. There's this drawing. It shows a Grecian warrior with a spear, facing right and taking a step. Ahead is a turtle, moving in the same direction. One: What would it suggest to you? Two: Have you seen anything like it recently?"

"No. I—say, what is this? By now I could have been home having a hot shower."

"Dr. Fuller left just such a drawing for me. Let's start off with the assumption it was significant. Only, I can't figure out what it means."

"Oddball, if you ask me."

"So, it's oddball. But does it suggest anything?"

He mulled over it, sucking pensively on his pipe. "Perhaps."

In the face of his continued silence, I asked, "Well, *what*?"

"Zeno."

"Zeno?"

"Zeno's Paradox. Achilles and the tortoise."

I snapped my fingers with a mental "But of course!" Achilles in pursuit of the tortoise, never able to overtake it because each time he covers half the gap, the turtle will move ahead by a proportionate distance.

"Can you think of any application the paradox might have in our work?" I asked excitedly.

Eventually he shrugged. "Not offhand. But then, I'm only responsible for the psychoprograming end of the operation. I wouldn't be able to speak authoritatively for the other phases."

"The upshot of the paradox, as I recall, is the assumption that all motion is an illusion."

"Basically."

"But that doesn't have any application at all, as far as I'm concerned." Evidently Zeno's Paradox wasn't what Fuller's drawing had been meant to suggest.

I reached for my drink, but Collingsworth stayed my arm. "I wouldn't attach seriousness to anything Fuller did during those last couple of weeks. He *was* acting rather peculiar, you know."

"Maybe he had a reason."

"No single reason could explain all the peculiarities."

"For instance?"

He pursed his lips. "I played chess with him two nights before he got killed. He hit the bottle the whole evening. Oddly, though, he didn't get a load on."

"Then he *was* concerned about something?"

"Nothing I could put my finger on, although I noticed he definitely wasn't himself. Kept going off on the philosophical end."

"About researching and improving human relations?"

"Oh, no—nothing like that. But—well, to be frank, he imagined that his work with Reactions was beginning to pay off with what he called 'basic discovery.'"

"What sort of discovery?"

"He wouldn't say."

Here was verification of a sort. Lynch, too, had spoken of Fuller's "secret"—information that he had hoped to save for me. Now I was *certain* Lynch had actually come to Siskin's party, that we *had* had our talk in the roof garden.

I lit my second cigarette.

"Why are you so interested in all this, Doug?"

"Because I don't think Fuller's death was an accident."

After a moment he said solemnly, "Look, son. I'm aware of all the elements that made up the Siskin-Fuller feud—allocation of sociological research time and all that. But really now, you don't think Siskin was so desperate as to want to bodily remove—"

"I didn't say that."

"Of course you didn't. And you'd better make certain you don't—ever. Siskin is a powerful, vindictive man."

I replaced my empty glass on the bar. "On the other hand, Fuller could find his way around blindfolded in the guts of the function generators. He'd be the last to walk into a high tension lead."

"A normal, not overly-eccentric Fuller, yes. Not Fuller as I knew him during those last couple of weeks."

Collingsworth finally got around to his straight shot. Then he thudded the glass on the bar and relit his pipe. The glow from the bowl made his features seem less intense. "I think I can guess what Fuller's 'basic discovery' was."

I tensed. "You can?"

"Sure. I'd bet it had a lot to do with his attitude toward the subjective reaction units in his simulator. If you remember, he more often than not referred to them as 'real people.'"

"But he was just being facetious."

"Was he? I can remember him saying, 'Damn it! We're not going to factor any analog pollsters into *this* setup!'"

I explained, "He planned it so that we wouldn't have to use interrogating units to poll opinion in our machine. He settled for a different system—audiovisual stimuli, such as billboards, handbills, contrived videocasts. We sample reaction by looking in on empathy-surveillance circuits."

"*Why* no pollsters in Fuller's counterfeit world?" he asked.

"Because actually it's more efficient without them. And we'll be getting a true reflection of social behavior minus the annoying factor of oral opinion sampling."

"That's the theory. But how many times did you hear Fuller say, 'I'm not going to have *my* little people harassed by any damned busybodies'?"

He had a point. Even I suspected that Fuller had fancied an unwarranted degree of sentience on the part of the ID units he was programing into his simulator.

Collingsworth spread his hands and smiled. "I believe Fuller's 'basic discovery' was that his reaction entities weren't merely ingenious circuits in a simulectronic complex, but instead were real, living, thinking personalities. In his opinion, I'm sure, they actually *existed*. In a solipsistic world, perhaps, but never suspecting that their past experiences were synthetic, that their universe wasn't a good, solid, firm, materialistic one."

"*You* don't believe anything like—"

His amused eyes relayed fitful reflections from a cigarette lighter that flared nearby. "My boy, I'm a pure psychologist—behaviorist leanings. My philosophy tracks that line closely. But you, Fuller, and all the other simulectronicists are a queer breed. When you start mixing psychology with electronics and sprinkle in a liberal dose of probability conditioning, you're bound to get some rather oddball convictions out of the mess. You can hardly stuff people into a machine without starting to wonder about the basic nature of both machines and people."

The discussion was getting far afield. I tried to steer it back on course. "I won't buy your assumption on Fuller's 'basic discovery.'

Because I think the discovery is the same thing Lynch was trying to tell me about."

"Lynch? Who's that?"

I drew back. Then I smiled, realizing that somehow he must have heard Jinx Fuller say she had never heard of Lynch. And now he was having his own little joke.

"Seriously," I went on, "if I hadn't believed Lynch's story about Fuller's 'secret,' I wouldn't have gone to the police."

"Lynch? The police? What's this all about?"

I began to suspect that he might be serious. "Avery, I'm not in the mood for horseplay. I'm talking about *Morton Lynch!*"

He shook his head stubbornly. "Don't know the man."

"Lynch!" I half shouted. "In charge of security at REIN!"

I pointed to a bronze loving cup behind the bar. "*That* Lynch! The one whose name is on that trophy for beating you in the ballistoboard tournament last year!"

Collingsworth beckoned across the bar and Limpy came over. "Will you tell Mr. Hall who has been chief of internal security at his establishment for the past five years?"

Limpy jerked his thumb toward a sour-faced, middle-aged man seated on the end stool. "Joe Gadsen."

"Now, Limpy, hand Mr. Hall that trophy."

I read the inscription: *Avery Collingsworth—June, 2033.*

The room lurched and whirled and the acrid smell of tobacco smoke seemed to surge up and envelop me like a fog. The music faded and the last thing I remembered was reaching out to steady myself with a grip on the bar.

I must not have passed out completely, though. For my next experience was that of bumping into someone on the staticstrip near the slowest pedestrian belt. I rebounded and leaned against a building— several blocks away from the smoke-easy.

It must have been another seizure—but one during which I had apparently remained in possession of myself. Avery probably hadn't even noticed anything was wrong. And here I was, suddenly conscious again, confounded and trembling, staring profoundly up into the early evening sky.

I thought helplessly of Lynch, his name on the trophy, Fuller's drawing. Had they all actually vanished? Or had I only fancied those occurrences? Why did order and reason seem suddenly to be tumbling down all around me?

Confounded, I crossed the pedistrip transfer platform and started for the opposite side of the street. Traffic was negligible and there were no air cars letting down on the nearby central landing island. That is, not until I got within twenty feet of it.

Then a vehicle came plunging out of the gathering dusk, emergency siren screaming. Apparently out of control, it shuddered fiercely as it slipped completely out of the down-guide beam, heading straight for me.

I dived for the high-speed pedistrip. The sudden motion of the belt almost hurled me back under the plummeting car. But I stuck, and managed, eventually, to sit up and glance back.

The car cushioned itself automatically with an emergency air blast that finally checked its momentum within an inch of the roadway.

If I had not gotten out of the way, the inner vanes would have left little in the way of identifiable remains.

✷FOUR✷

A SUCCESSION OF NIGHTMARES IN which everything I reached for crumbled in my grip blocked restful slumber until the early morning hours. Consequently I overslept and had to skip breakfast.

Flying downtown, however, I avoided the heavy traffic levels, at the expense of additional delay, while my thoughts stalled on the near accident of the night before. Did it fit into the general pattern? Had the air car purposely gone out of control?

I shrugged off my suspicion. The accident *couldn't* have been intentional. On the other hand, Dr. Fuller had met with a fatal accident that couldn't have been contrived either. And there was Lynch's disappearance. Had there been some unguessable purpose behind that too? And how was it that three of Lynch's close acquaintances now appeared never to have heard of him?

Had all these incredible developments stemmed from some obscure information Fuller had passed on to Lynch? Knowledge that had instantly marked first the original, then the subsequent possessor?

I tried to keep the pieces in some sort of rational perspective, but couldn't. The altered plaque on the trophy kept surging to the foreground of my attention, bringing with it a now nonexistent red-ink drawing and a weasel-like little man who had sat smugly on his smoke-easy stool while Limpy proclaimed him REIN's security chief.

It all smacked of nothing less than—the extraphysical. I had avoided that suggestion as long as I could. But what else?

At any rate, at least one thing seemed not unlikely: Fuller and

Lynch had become involved with "secret information" or "basic dis-covery"—call it whatever you will. What would happen if *I* acquired those data? Or even continued to show an interest in it? Was the air car incident just a foretaste?

I guided my own car down into the REIN parking lot and sent it skittering to its assigned space. As soon as I cut the engine I caught the sounds of turmoil in front of the building.

Negotiating the corner, I ducked a length of pipe hurtling through the air toward a first-floor window. But it lost its momentum in a shower of sparks, then mushed to the ground along the fringe of a repulsion screen.

The number of reaction monitor pickets had tripled. But they were still orderly. The trouble was coming, rather, from a surly crowd that had collected in defiance of a police riot squad.

Down the block, on the transfer platform, a red-faced man was shouting into a voice amplifier:

"Down with Reactions! We haven't had a depression in thirty years! Machine sampling will mean total economic collapse!"

The riot squad sergeant came over. "You're Douglas Hall?"

When I nodded, he added, "I'll escort you through."

He switched on his portable screen generator and I felt the tingling embrace of the repulsion field as it built up around us.

"You don't seem to be trying to break this up," I complained, follow-ing him toward the entrance.

"You got ample protection. Anyway, if we don't let them work off their steam, they'll get even hotter."

Inside, everything was normal. There was no indication whatever that not a hundred feet away reaction monitor sympathizers were stirring up a hornets' nest. But the amount of crash-priority work on the day's agenda required just that degree of indifference.

I went directly to personnel. Under the L's in the filing cabinet, there was no folder for Morton Lynch.

Under the G's I found "Gadsen, Joseph M.—Director, Internal Se-curity." The employment application was dated September 11, 2029—five years ago. And the file showed he had been hired in his present position two weeks later.

"Something wrong, Mr. Hall?"

I turned to face the filing clerk. "This material up to date?"

"Yes sir," she said proudly. "I go through it every week."

"Have we had any complaints on—Joe Gadsen?"

"Oh, no sir. Only fitness testimonials. He gets along with everybody. Isn't that right, Mr. Gadsen?" She smiled sweetly at a point beyond my shoulder.

I spun around. The weasel-faced character was standing there.

He grinned. "Somebody has a beef against me, Doug?"

I didn't say anything for a moment. Finally I managed a weak "No."

"That's good," he replied, obviously regarding the whole thing as superficial. "Incidentally, Helen says thanks for the mess of trout you sent down from the lake. If you're not doing anything Friday evening, come on over and break bread. Anyway, Junior wants to hear more about simulectronics. You've got him fairly fascinated with the subject."

Joe Gadsen, Helen, Junior—the words resounded hollowly within my ear like the exotic names of strange natives on some yet-to-be-discovered world halfway across the galaxy. And his mention of the trout—why, I hadn't caught a single fish during the entire month at the lake! At least, I didn't remember catching any.

There was one ultimate test that occurred to me. I left Gadsen and the file clerk gaping at each other and swept down the corridor to Chuck Whitney's bailiwick in the function generating department. I found him with his head buried in the innards of his main data-integrator. I thumped him on the shoulder and he came up for air.

"Chuck, I—"

"Yes, Doug—what is it?" His friendly, tanned face reflected amusement, then uncertainty over my too-obvious hesitancy.

He ran a hand back over a mat of dark hair that was so compressed in its unmanageable crimpiness that it was reminiscent of the crewcut and flattop which haven't been in style for over a generation. Then, concerned, he asked, "You got trouble?"

"It's about—Morton Lynch," I said reluctantly. "Ever hear of him?"

"Who?"

"Lynch," I repeated, suddenly hopeless. "Morton, the security—oh, never mind. Forget it."

A moment later I drew up at the entrance to my reception room and was greeted with a cheerful "Good *morning*, Mr. Hall."

I did a double take at the receptionist. Miss Boykins was gone. In her place sat Dorothy Ford, strikingly blond and alert as she regarded me with coy amusement. "Surprised?" she murmured.

"Where's Miss Boykins?"

"Mr. Siskin calleth and she respondeth. She's now in the comforting folds of the Inner Establishment—content, we should hope, with her considerable nearness to the Great Little One."

I went over. "Is this a permanent arrangement?"

She coaxed a stray hair back away from her temple. But somehow she didn't appear quite as frivolous or inefficient as she had at Siskin's party. She glanced down at her hands and said suggestively, "Oh, I'm sure you won't mind the change, Doug?"

But I did. And possibly I indicated as much by continuing on into my office with an uninspired, "I'll get used to it." I didn't appreciate the fact that Siskin was shifting his pawns around the board and that I was one of them. It was obvious now that he was going to have his way when it came to assigning functions to the environment simulator. And I had no doubt he would reject my recommendation for partial use of the system in sociological research—just as he had been about to give Fuller a determined "No" on the same matter.

In my case, though, there was to be appeasement of a sort—appeasement and, evidently, some form of supposedly interesting diversion. Miss Boykins, admittedly, was not quite the antithesis of homeliness, but she was efficient and pleasant. The versatile Dorothy Ford, in contrast, could serve a multiplicity of purposes—not the least significant of which would undoubtedly be "keeping an eye" on me in behalf of the Siskin Establishment.

Such mental exercise didn't occupy my attention very long, however, as the Lynch enigma drew me back like a magnet.

I went to work on the videophone and, within seconds, had Lieutenant McBain on the screen.

After identifying myself, I said, "About my complaint on Morton Lynch—"

"What department did you want?"

"Missing Persons, of course. I—"

"When did you file your complaint? What was it about?"

I swallowed heavily. But his reaction wasn't something I hadn't anticipated. "Morton Lynch," I said haltingly. "At the Siskin party. The disappearance. You came out to Reactions and—"

"I'm sorry, Mr. Hall, but you must have me confused with someone else. This department has no such complaint on file."

Minutes later I was still staring at the dead screen.

Then I bolted forward in my chair and pulled open the top desk drawer. The copy of the *Evening Press* that I had set aside was still there. I turned anxiously to the amusement page and read the final item in Stan Walters' column.

It was a barbed, sarcastic appraisal of the Community Theater's latest production.

Not a word about Morton Lynch and Siskin's penthouse party.

The intercom buzzed itself hoarse before I finally pressed the lever without even glancing at the screen. "Yes, Miss Ford?"

"Mr. Siskin is here to see you."

Again, he was not alone. This time he brought in an impeccably dressed man whose very proportions made Dorothy's "dapper little doll" seem even more minuscule by comparison.

"Doug," Siskin said excitedly, "I want you to meet someone who isn't here! Understand? He has *never been* here. After we leave, it's as though he didn't exist, as far as you're concerned."

I lunged up, almost knocking my chair over in recognition of the parallel between what he was proposing and what had happened to Lynch.

"Douglas Hall, Wayne Hartson," he offered, climaxing his build-up.

I extended an unsteady hand and it was immediately locked in a fierce grip.

"I'll be working with Hall?" Hartson asked.

"Only if we get everything ironed out. Only if Doug understands that what we're doing is best."

Hartson frowned. "I thought you had everything cleared away within your own organization."

"Oh, I *do!*" Siskin assured him.

Then I made the connection. Wayne Hartson, one of the strongest political figures in the country.

"Without Hartson," Siskin went on almost in a whisper, "the administration couldn't operate. Of course, his connections are all under the surface, since he appears only to be handling liaison work between the party and the government."

Dorothy signaled and her image came through on the intercom. "Certified Reaction Monitor Number 3471-C on the videophone for Mr. Hall."

Anger flared in Siskin's eyes as he thrust himself in front of the box. "Tell—"

But the girl's face had already been replaced by that of the pollster. "I'm conducting a survey on male preferences in Christmas gifts," he disclosed.

"Then," Siskin growled, "this *isn't* a priority sampling?"

"No, sir. But—"

"Mr. Hall declines to answer. Just pick up the tape on this call and go file for the penalty."

Siskin switched off and the screen went dead on the man's gathering smile. Reaction monitors didn't at all mind claiming their share of the refusal fine.

"About Mr. Hartson," Siskin resumed, "I was pointing out that the administration couldn't get along without him."

"I've heard of Mr. Hartson," I said, bracing myself for what I knew was coming.

Hartson pulled up a chair, crossed his legs, and donned a patient expression.

Siskin paced, glancing occasionally at me. "We've gone over this before, Doug, and I know you don't quite see it my way. But good God, boy, Reactions can become the biggest thing in the country! Then, after we've recovered our investment, I'll build you another simulator that you can use only for your research.

"It's coming, Doug—the one-party system. We *can't* hold it off. And I'm not too sure it isn't right for the country. But the point is— Reactions can get in *on the bottom* in the transition!"

Hartson spoke up. "We can pull it off in the next two or three years by squeezing the other party completely out and siphoning off its top talent—if we play our cards right," he said frankly.

Siskin leaned over the desk. "And do you know what's going to tell them which cards to play—in every national and local election and on every issue? *The simulator I built for you!*"

I felt a little sickened over his candid enthusiasm. "What's in it for you?"

"What's in it for us?" He resumed his vigorous pacing, his eyes wide and restless. "I'll tell you, son. We can look forward to the time when the entire complex of opinion sampling, of *oral* reaction monitoring, will be legislated out of existence as an insufferable public nuisance."

Hartson coughed for attention. "Reactions will be sitting pretty with its secret process. There'll still be need for opinion sampling, on as universal a plane as ever. But," he shook his head in feigned concern, "I don't see how that need will be satisfied unless we institute a federal franchise for REIN."

"Don't you see, Doug?" Siskin gripped the desk. "There'll be Siskin-Hall simulators in every city! *Your* reaction units will be calling the shots! It'll mean a whole new world! And then, after all the groundwork is laid, you'll have an entire corps of simulectronic foundations researching ways to shine up the world and make it fair and just and humane!"

Perhaps I should have told him he could look for another simulectronicist. But what good would that have done? If, as Fuller had believed, Siskin and the party were plotting treachery on an unprecedented level, what purpose would I serve by removing myself from a strategic position?

"What do you want me to do?" I asked.

Siskin grinned. "Go on with your present setup. Get squared away for a few commercial contracts. That'll give us a chance to test the potential of the system. Meanwhile, you can be thinking of reprograming the machine completely, converting it to a politically-oriented environment."

Dorothy cut in on the intercom. "Mr. Hall, Mr. Whitney is programing in that new batch of reaction units. He wants to know if you can come down there."

On the way to the function generating department, I encountered Avery Collingsworth in the corridor.

"I've just given Whitney a final okay on the psychological traits for those forty-seven new ID units," he said. "Here's a rundown, in case you'd like to check them over."

I refused the clipboard he offered. "That won't be necessary. I haven't questioned your judgment thus far."

"I could slip up, you know." He smiled.

"You won't."

He hesitated and I tried to break away without letting him think I was uneasy over what had happened at the smoke-easy.

He touched my arm solicitously. "You feeling all right now?"

"Sure." I forced a casual laugh. "About last night at Limpy's—I guess I just had a few too many while waiting for you."

He flashed a relieved grin, then continued down the hall.

Outside Whitney's department, I pulled up sharply and slumped against the wall. There it was again—seas roaring in my ears, pulse pounding against my temples. But I fought off unconsciousness. Finally the walls steadied and I stood there tense and fearful. Scanning the corridor to see whether anyone had witnessed the seizure, I continued on to the function generating room.

Chuck Whitney, emerging from a maintenance recess, was elated. "All forty-seven ID units successfully integrated!" he exclaimed.

"They took it in stride?"

"Not a single shock withdrawal. Current simulator population: nine thousand one hundred and thirty-six."

We took the lift to one of the ID "wards" on the second floor. I walked down the nearest row of reactor storage units. At the beginning of the stretch containing the newly-added entities, I paused, quietly impressed.

Each console gave confident assurance, through a whisper of whirring memory drums, a clatter of synaptic relays, the rhythms of its servo mechanisms, that the counterfeit life within was vigorous and orderly, that cognitive circuits were being properly stimulated.

I watched the myriad function-positive lights blinking on two of the panels. Corresponding bulbs seemed to be flicking on and off in perfect harmony. And I could imagine that pair of reaction units in analogous contact. A young man and woman, maybe. Being borne arm-in-arm on a pedistrip. Perhaps even thinking related thoughts as they built their own structure of optional experience upon the foundation of reality we had given them.

I understood, without reservation now, how Fuller had been moved to speak of the characters in his simulator as "my little people."

Chuck interrupted my thoughts. "I can cut you in on either a direct empathy or personal surveillance circuit," he suggested, "if you'd care to run a spot check."

✠

But the wall speaker hummed abruptly with Dorothy Ford's voice. "Mr. Hall, there's a Police Captain Farnstock here to see you. He's waiting in the function room."

We took the lift down and Farnstock, extending his credentials, came forward to meet us.

"Hall?" he asked, staring at Whitney.

"No," Chuck corrected, "I'm Whitney. This is Hall."

I tensed, but only momentarily, at his failure to recognize me. After all, hadn't Lieutenant McBain, only an hour earlier, also acted as though he had never heard of me before?

Chuck went out of the room and the captain said, "I'd like to ask a few questions about Dr. Fuller's death."

"Why?" I lifted a curious eyebrow. "The coroner said it was accidental, didn't he?"

The captain's impassive, thickset face sagged patronizingly. "We never let it go at that. I'll be frank, Mr. Hall. It's possible that what happened to Fuller *wasn't* accidental. I understand you were on leave at the time."

I started mentally. Not because I was being questioned in connection with what the police *now* thought was a murder. Rather because it seemed to me that some of the pieces might be falling together in a totally unanticipated manner.

Fuller was dead; Lynch, gone. Forgotten too. All because of some "basic" information whose nature I was now trying to learn. In the process I had almost been killed. Now this—a suddenly revitalized police investigation. Was it a tactful maneuver to get me out of the way? But how? And who could be responsible?

"Well?" Farnstock coaxed.

"I told you. I was at my cabin on the lake."

"What do you mean, you told me?"

I swallowed. "Nothing. I was at my cabin."

"Anybody with you?"

"No."

"Then you don't have any way of proving you were elsewhere when Fuller died. Or that you were ever at your cabin at all."

"Why should I prove anything? Fuller was my best friend."

He smiled insincerely. "Like a father?"

He glanced around, as though to take in the entire building, not just the function generating room. "You're doing all right now, aren't you? Technical director, A chance for part ownership in one of the hottest enterprises of the twenty-first century."

Calmly, I said "There's a supply post half a mile from the cabin where I picked up the things I needed—on a day-to-day basis almost. The account tapes will show how often and when things were charged to my particular biocapacitance."

"We'll see," he said warily. "In the meantime, don't be where we wouldn't think of looking for you."

✳FIVE✳

IT WAS ANOTHER COUPLE OF days before I could find time to run a spot check on Simulacron-3. Besides being shackled with work, I had to appease Siskin by jotting down a few preliminary plans for converting the simulectronic complex to a politically-oriented base.

Meanwhile, I could only flounder in speculation over the renewed police investigation. Was it an independent development? Or was Siskin merely pulling strings to demonstrate what might happen if I should decide not to go along with him and the party?

At one point, during a videophone conversation with Siskin, I even broached the matter of Captain Farnstock's visit. And I felt that my suspicion was vindicated when he showed little surprise over the sudden police interest in Fuller's death.

Making it subtly clear that it would be to my advantage to remain in his favor, he said, "If they start breathing down your neck, just let me know."

I decided then to test him on yet another point. "You can hardly blame the police for sticking with it," I said guardedly. "After all, Lynch kept suggesting Fuller's death wasn't accidental."

"Lynch? Lynch?"

I pushed ahead boldly but ambiguously. "Morton Lynch. The man who did a fade-out at your party."

"Lynch? Fade-out? What *are* you talking about, son?"

His reaction was sincere. And it suggested that Siskin, like everybody else except me, had lost all memory of the man who had vanished from his roof garden. Or he was a damned good actor.

"Lynch," I lied expediently, "was some character who kept kidding me about knocking off Fuller to get his job."

When I finally found time for the spot simulator check Whitney had suggested, I was surprised to find myself approaching the experience with more than casual anticipation.

Chuck accompanied me into the "peephole" room and led me to the nearest reclining couch. "What kind of look-see will you have?" he asked, grinning. "Surveillance circuit?"

"No. Just a plain empathic coupling."

"Any particular ID unit?"

"You pick him."

Obviously he already had. "How about 'D. Thompson'—IDU-7412?"

"Suits me. What's his line?"

"Van pilot. We'll pick him up on a delivery job. Okay?"

"Shoot."

He lowered the transfer helmet on my head, then joked, "Give me any trouble and I'll arrange a shot of surge voltage."

I didn't laugh. Fuller had theorized that runaway gain in the modulator *could* kick back with a reciprocal transfer. Just as the observer's ego was temporarily planted within the ID's storage unit, so might the latter's sweep up and impress itself upon the brain of the observer in a violent, instant exchange.

It wasn't that the reciprocal transfer couldn't be reversed later. But if something should happen to the *image* of the ID unit meanwhile, it would theoretically be curtains for the trapped observer.

Relaxing against the leather padding, I watched Chuck cross over to the transfer panel, make a few final adjustments, then reach for the activator switch.

There was a brief, sharp twisting of all my senses—a kaleidoscopic flare of light, a screeching blast of sound, a sudden assault of impossible tastes and smells and tactile sensations.

Then I was through, on the other side. And there was that fleeting moment of fear and confusion as my conceptual processes readjusted to the perceptual faculties of D. Thompson—IDU-7412.

I sat at the controls of an air van leisurely watching the analog city slip by below. I was sensitive even to the steady rise and fall of my

(Thompson's) chest and the warmth of the sun that blazed through the plexidome.

But it was a passive association. I could only look, listen, feel. I had no motor authority. Nor was there any way the subjective unit could be aware of the empathic coupling.

I slipped down to the lower, subvocal level and encountered his flow of conscious thought: I was annoyed that I had fallen behind schedule. But, what the hell, I (IDU-7412) didn't give a damn. Why, I could draw down twice as much with any other vanning firm.

Satisfied with the completeness of the coupling, I (Doug Hall) pulled back from total to perceptive empathy and saw through Thompson's eyes as he glanced at the man in the other seat.

And I wondered whether his helper was a valid ID unit, or merely one of the "props." Of the latter we had supplied hundreds of thousands in order to pad out the simulated environment.

Impatiently, I waited for Chuck to feed in the test stimulus. I was looking forward to getting away early that afternoon, since I had a date with Jinx at her home for dinner and a glance at Dr. Fuller's notes.

The stimulus finally came. Thompson had been staring at it for fully ten seconds before I recognized it for what it was.

On the roof of one of the tall buildings below, a horizontal billboard's high-intensity xenon vapor lights were repeatedly blinking:

SOROPMAN'S SCOTCH—MELLOW, SMOOTH
CAN YOU THINK OF A BETTER DISTILLERS' PRODUCT?

It was a gimmick for prodding our subjective units into expressing opinion. Thompson, who had been exposed to the simulectronic equivalent of Soropman's Scotch over what, to him, had appeared to be a number of years, reacted reflexively.

Damned rotgut! I (IDU-7412) thought. *It might not be too bad if it was aged enough to take out the sting. But Scotch—in a bottle shaped like a bowling ball?*

Meanwhile, all other visual advertising media throughout the analog city were flashing the same message.

And reactions of thousands of ID entities were being sifted out, analyzed, herded into the master output-register. There they would be sorted, stored and indexed. Merely the flick of a switch would produce complete categorical breakdowns by age, sex, occupation, political affiliation and the like.

In the space of but a few seconds, Fuller's total environment simulator had accomplished what otherwise would have required a month-long effort by an army of certified reaction monitors.

What happened next took me completely off guard and it was fortunate that the empathy coupling was a one-way arrangement. Or D. Thompson would have known he was not alone in his astonishment.

A fierce streak of lightning crashed down out of the clear sky. Three huge fireballs blazed high overhead. Clouds appeared from nowhere, expanding explosively until they blotted out almost all of the daylight, and unleashed lashing torrents of hail. Spontaneous flames enveloped two lesser buildings below.

Perplexed, I rejected the possibility that Chuck was clowning with the background props. Although something like this could, without prohibitive strain, be shrugged off by the ID units as a "freak of nature," Whitney wouldn't take the chance of disturbing the equilibrium of our delicately balanced analog community.

There was only one other possibility: Something had gone wrong with the simulectronic complex! Imbalance, breakdown, faulty generation, even a simple short—all would be automatically rationalized by the system as more or less "natural" equivalents of errant electronic forces. There had been a foul-up somewhere along the line, but Chuck hadn't retrieved me because withdrawal from a look-see coupling had to be either voluntary or at the end of the programed interval. Otherwise a major portion of the subject's ego might be irretrievably lost.

Then Thompson's eyes swept across the horizontal billboard and I sensed his puzzled reaction to the anomalous message that was now being flashed out by the xenon lights:

DOUG! COME BACK! EMERGENCY!

Instantly, I broke the empathic coupling and swam up through wrenching transition to my own subjective orientation. The peephole department was a bedlam of scurrying figures, shouting voices, stifling heat, pungent smells of burning insulation.

Chuck, working desperately with a fire extinguisher at the control console, glanced toward my couch.

"You're back!" he shouted. "Thank God! We might have gotten a current surge at any minute!"

Then he snapped off the master switch. The crackling sound of electrical arcing stopped abruptly, as though someone had closed a door on it. But fierce, blazing light continued to pour out of the console's ventilation louvers.

I cast the helmet aside. "What happened?"

"Somebody planted a thermite charge in the modulator!"

"Just now?"

"I don't know. I stepped out after I plugged you in. If I hadn't come back in time, you might have been cremated!"

Siskin accepted the thermite charge episode with surprising composure—too calmly, I thought. Within minutes, it seemed, he was at Reactions, surveying the damage and nodding over our assurance that we wouldn't be delayed more than a day or two.

As to who had been responsible for the treachery, he had his answer ready and emphasized it by ramming his fist into his palm. "Those damned reaction monitors! One of them managed to get in here!"

Joe Gadsen vigorously denied that possibility. "Our security measures are foolproof, Mr. Siskin."

Siskin glowered. "Then it was done *on the inside!* I want everybody double-screened all over again!"

Back in my office, I paced in front of the window, watching the once-again orderly scene outside. Only pollster pickets. No more surging mobs. But how long would it stay that way? And what was the common denominator underlying the reaction monitors, the thermite attack and all the other impossible things that had happened?

Somehow I was certain there had to be a fundamental relationship among all the bizarre occurrences of the past week or so—Fuller's death, Lynch's disappearance, Lynch's "total erasure" from the whole web of former experience, Fuller's bequest of a now nonexistent Achilles sketch, an altered plaque on a trophy behind Limpy's bar, the off-and-on-again police investigation.

Take the thermite bombing: It had ostensibly been an aggressive action by the Association of Reaction Monitors against the institution that was threatening that group's continued existence. But *was* it that? Or had it been intended, instead, *for me?*

Who was behind it? Certainly not Siskin. For even though he might conceivably want me removed, he already had the means of achieving that through the police investigation which he was manipulating.

Then, as I paused to stare out the window, a novel possibility suggested itself: *many* of the perplexing effects might have been aimed indirectly *at the environment simulator itself!*

Fuller's death, Lynch's disappearance, the thermite charge, my near-accidents—a planned campaign to eliminate the only two simulectronicists capable of insuring REIN's success?

The finger pointed back at the Association of Reaction Monitors. But, again, logic shouted it couldn't be ARM. It had to be some agency with either extraphysical powers or a convincing means of simulating them.

I couldn't shake the succession of enigmas out of my mind, not even while sharing a quiet and thoughtful meal with Jinx that evening.

We had eaten in silence for fully ten minutes when I was drawn from my own reflections by the realization that there was no reason for *her* to be so deep in thought.

"Jinx."

She started and dropped her fork. It clattered on her plate and she smiled awkwardly, then laughed. "You frightened me."

But I had hardly whispered her name. "Anything wrong?"

She wore a shimmering, cream-colored frock that retreated far below her shoulders. In so doing, it presented a considerable expanse of tanned skin as a backdrop for her long, dark hair.

"I'm all right," she said. "I was thinking about Dad."

She glanced toward the study and her hands came up to hide her face. I went around the table to offer condolence, but only stood there, confused over the realization that something was not quite right. I could understand her bereavement, since she and her father had had only each other. But this display of emotion was a striking throwback to the mid-twentieth century.

Things had been different before enlightenment had modified the attitude toward death and swept away the vicious cruelty of the funeral convention. In those days, proof of death had to be established on a practical plane. Those who attended wakes and funeral services saw and believed. And they went away convinced that the loved one was

actually beyond this life and that there would be no complications aris-
ing from a supposedly dead person showing up again. That the close
ones also went away nursing traumatic wounds made little difference.

As soon as technology asserted itself, however, proof of death was
abundantly available even in such crude techniques as fingerprinting,
biocapacitance indexing, and cortical resonance checks. And the deepest
wound the family suffered was that of being told there had been a death
and the body had been disposed of.

What I'm trying to point out is that since I had known Jinx to be
a normal girl, her present extreme desolation was far out of character.

And as she led me into the study a moment later, I wondered
abruptly whether she was merely letting me *believe* her bereavement
had been responsible for the tearful outburst. Was she concealing a far
more profound cause of distress?

She gestured toward Fuller's desk. "Help yourself while I go resur-
face my face."

Pensively, I watched her weave from the room, tall and graceful and
lovely even despite inflamed eyes.

She stayed away long enough for me to go through Fuller's scant
professional effects. But only two things caught my attention. First,
in the surprisingly few notes that had been spread out across the desk
and stored in two of its drawers, some of the memoranda were missing. How did I know? Well, Fuller had told me on several occasions
that he was working at home on the consequences of simulectronics in
terms of human understanding. There was not a word to be found on
that subject.

Second, one drawer of the desk—the one in which he had kept his
important notations—had been forced open.

As for the notes themselves, there was nothing to attract my interest. Not that I had really expected to find anything.

Jinx returned and sat tensely, unsmiling, on the edge of the couch,
slender hands cupped around her knees. Her face had recaptured its
freshness. But there seemed to be a certain guarded determination in
the firm, smooth lines of her mouth.

"Is everything just like Dr. Fuller left it?" I asked.

"Nothing's been touched."

"There are some notes missing," I said, watching carefully for her reactions.

Her eyes widened. "How do you know?"

"He told me about something he was working on. I can't find any mention of it."

She glanced away—uneasily?—then back at me. "Oh, he disposed of a lot of papers, just last week."

"Where?"

"He incinerated them."

I indicated the forced drawer. "And what about this?"

"I—" Then she smiled and came over to the desk. "Is this a sort of inquisition?"

Relaxing, I said, "I'm just trying to pick up the pieces of some research odds and ends."

"It can't be that important, can it?" But before I could answer, she suggested impulsively, "Let's go for a drive, Doug."

I took her back to the couch and we sat side by side. "Just a few more questions. That broken lock?"

"Dad lost his key. That was about three weeks ago. He pried the drawer open with a knife."

That, I knew, was a lie. A year earlier I had helped Fuller install a biocapacitance trigger on the lock so he could open the drawer without his key, which he had often misplaced.

She rose. "If we're going to take that drive, I'll get a wrap."

"About that sketch your father drew—"

"Sketch?"

"The drawing of Achilles and the tortoise, in red ink—at his office. You didn't take it, did you?"

"I didn't even see it."

Not only had she noticed the sketch, but I had stood behind her watching her study it for some time.

I decided to toss a shocker at her, just to see what sort of effect it might have. "Jinx, what I'm trying to find out is whether your father *really* died accidentally."

Her mouth fell open and she stepped back. "Oh, Doug, you're not *serious*? You mean somebody might have—killed him?"

"I think so. I also thought there might be something in his notes indicating who and why."

"But nobody would have wanted to do anything like that!"

She was silent a moment. "And if you're right, you could be in danger yourself! Oh, Doug, you've got to forget about it!"

"Don't you want to see the guilty person exposed?"

"I don't know." She hesitated. "I'm frightened. I don't want anything to happen to you."

I noticed with interest that she hadn't suggested going to the police. "Why do you think anything's going to happen to me?"

"I—oh, Doug, I'm confused and afraid."

A brilliant lunar disk transformed the car's plexidome into a shimmering silver cupola that splashed soft radiance on the figure of the girl seated beside me.

Reticent and distant, eyes boring ahead as the road unfolded before the car's air cushion, she seemed like a fragile Dresden that might crumble beneath the feathery assault of moonlight.

She was withdrawn in thought now, but she had not been only a few minutes earlier. Then she had pleaded with me, almost desperately, to forget that her father might have been murdered.

And I was only all the more confounded. It was almost as though she were standing as a shield between me and whatever had befallen her father. And I couldn't avoid the impression that she was extending a protective cloak over whoever had been responsible.

I laid my hand upon hers. "Jinx, are you in trouble?"

Her normal reaction would have been to ask whatever had given me that idea. But she only said, "No, of course not."

The words were a calm resolution, a dedication to the course she had elected. And I knew I could push no further along that avenue. I would have to look elsewhere, even though Jinx represented a direct route to my objective.

Then I retreated into my own shell of thought, switching onto automatic and letting the car guide itself along the unfamiliar, deserted country road. There were only two possible explanations that would cover all the incongruous circumstances. One: Some vast, malevolent agency of a capacity both fierce and unguessable was pursuing an unfathomable course. Two: Nothing at all of an extraordinary nature had occurred—except in my mind.

But I couldn't shake off the insidious notion that some brutish, mystical force was determined to discourage me from pinning down the cause of Fuller's death, while it held out the implied promise at the same time that if I quit flouting its authority, as both it and Jinx seemed to want me to, everything would be all right.

I *wanted* things to go right. Glancing over at the girl, I realized how feverishly I longed for normality. She was beautiful in the moonlight, like a warm beacon inviting me to cast off my distress and accept the ordinary things.

But she wasn't ordinary. She was something very special.

Seeming to sense my thoughts, she moved next to me, took my arm in hers, and laid her head on my shoulder.

"There's *so* much in life, isn't there, Doug?" she said with a strange mixture of melancholy and hope in her voice.

"As much as you want to find in it," I answered.

"And what do *you* want to find?"

I thought of her, exploding into my existence at a time when I so critically needed someone like her.

"While I was away I never stopped thinking of you," she said. "I felt like a silly, frustrated child all along. But I never stopped."

I waited for the silken flow of words to resume, but heard only the sound of deep breathing. She was asleep. And on her cheeks twin rivers of quicksilver spangled in the moonlight.

She was running away from something, just as I was. But I knew then that even though we perhaps shared the same despair, there was no way we could communicate it to each other, because, for some incomprehensible reason, that was the way she wanted it.

The car headed up a hillside, bathing the slope with its lights and revealing a section of the country I had never seen before.

We topped the hill and a blast of icy terror tore at my chest. I hit the braking stud and we came smoothly, swiftly to a halt.

Jinx stirred but didn't awaken.

I sat there for an eternity, staring incredulously ahead.

The road ended a hundred feet away.

On each side of the strip, the very earth itself dropped off into an impenetrable barrier of stygian blackness.

Out there were no stars, no moonlight—only the nothingness within nothingness that might be found beyond the darkest infinity.

✖ SIX ✖

LATER, I REALIZED I SHOULD have awakened Jinx at the climax of that reason-shattering drive into the country. Then, by her reaction, I would have known whether half of all creation had blinked out of existence or whether I had merely imagined that effect. But I only sat there fighting off another partial lapse of consciousness. When I finally overcame the seizure and managed to look up again, the road was there, stretching normally into the distance, flanked by serene fields and rolling hills which stood out sharply in the moonlight.

There it was again—the redeeming circumstance. The road had disappeared. But it *couldn't* have, because there it was. Similarly, Lynch had vanished. But all evidence indicated he had never existed. There was no way I could prove I had seen a sketch of Achilles and the tortoise. But the compensating possibility was that it had never been drawn in the first place.

It wasn't until the following afternoon that Chuck Whitney came up with a sufficiently challenging simulectronic problem to rescue my thoughts from their treadmill of unreason.

He entered my office through the private staff door, dropped into a chair, and swung his heels up on the desk. "Well, we finally got the look-see modulator back in operation."

I turned from the window, where I had been staring out at the reaction monitor pickets. "You don't seem very happy about it."

"We lost two whole days."

"We'll make it up."

"Of course we will." He smiled wearily. "But that environmental breakdown scared the hell out of our Contact Unit down there. For a while I thought P. Ashton would go irrational and have to be yanked."

I glanced uncomfortably at the floor. "Ashton is the only weak link in Fuller's system. No analog mentality can stand up against the knowledge that he's merely a complex of electrical charges in a simulated reality."

"I don't like it either. But Fuller was right. We've *got* to have a dependable observer down there. So many things could start going wrong without our finding out about it for days."

It was a problem that had mired my thoughts for weeks, eventually driving me to take that month's leave so I could come to grips with my dissatisfaction. Somehow I couldn't shake off the conviction that permitting a Contact Unit to know he is nothing more than an electronically simulated entity was the height of ruthlessness.

Suddenly decided, I said, "Chuck, we're going to junk that system as soon as possible. Instead we'll set up a surveillance staff. We'll do all our observing through the medium of direct projection into the simulator. No more P. Ashtons."

His expression shifted into a relieved grin. "I'll start setting up the staff. Meanwhile, we have just one more problem. We're going to lose Cau No."

"Who?"

"Cau No. He's the 'average immigrant' in our population. A Burmese. IDU-4313. Ashton reported half an hour ago that he attempted suicide."

"Why?"

"As best I could get it, astrological considerations required as much. That upheaval in the environment convinced him doomsday was imminent."

"That's easily taken care of. Remotivate him. If he's developed a suicide urge, just program it out."

Chuck rose and went to the window. "It's not that simple. Ranting and raving about the meteors and the storm and fires, he attracted quite a crowd. Sold them on the idea that all those freaks of nature couldn't happen at the same time. Ashton says a whole slew of ID entities are wondering about the upheaval."

"Oh. That's bad."

He shrugged. "By itself it would probably wash off. But if something else like that should happen, we may have a lot of irrational reaction units running around. Best thing to do is shut down Simulacron-3 for another couple of days and wipe off the storm and fires completely. Cau No is going to have to go too. His 'obsession' is too deep."

After he had gone, I settled down at the desk and, without realizing it, soon had my pen in hand. Absently, I tried to duplicate Fuller's drawing of the Grecian warrior and the turtle.

But I soon tossed the pen aside, irritated over the defiant incomprehensibility of the sketch. My description of the drawing had suggested something to Avery Collingsworth, I remembered: Zeno's Paradox. But I was certain that Fuller's sketch had been meant to imply neither the paradox nor its resultant proposition that motion is impossible.

Attentively, I turned over on my tongue the phrase "All motion is an illusion."

Then I realized there was *one* frame of reference in which all motion *is* an illusion—*in the* simulator *itself!* The subjective units fancy themselves operating within a physical environment. Yet as they move around they actually go nowhere. All that happens when a reactional entity such as Cau No "walks" from one building to another, for instance, is that simulectronic currents bias a grid and transducers feed the illusive "experiences" onto a memory drum.

Had Fuller wanted me to recognize *that* principle in the drawing? But what had he been trying to say?

Then I lurched from the chair.

Cau No!

Cau No was the key! It shone through in stark clarity now. The sketch was meant simply to suggest the word "Zeno"!

In referring to the characters in our simulator, the Reactions staff had adopted the informal practice of identifying them by their last names and first initials.

Thus, Cau No became "C. No"—almost the phonetic equivalent of "Zeno"!

Of course! Fuller had had vital information to pass on to me. And he had employed the most secretive way of doing it. He had impressed it on a reactional unit's storage drum. And he had left a coded message identifying the unit!

I sprinted through the reception room, leaving a curious Dorothy Ford staring after me, frozen in the motions of restoring body to the sweep of her pageboy.

I went bounding up the stairs, berating myself for not knowing which ID ward housed Cau No's storage console.

After scanning the wall indexes in two wards, I charged into a third—only to collide with Whitney and knock him over backwards. His tool box spilled its contents on the floor.

"The Cau No cabinet!" I demanded. "Where is it?"

He gestured over his shoulder. "Last one on the left. But it's dead. I just wiped the circuits clean."

Back in my office, I braced myself against the desk and cringed before another vertiginous assault. Head pounding, perspiration filming my face, the drone of a thousand wasps drumming in my ears, I tried to hold back unconsciousness. When the room finally stabilized itself, I fell into the chair, exhausted and despondent.

It was almost incredibly coincidental that Cau No should have been deprogramed just minutes before I had solved the enigma of the drawing. For a moment it even seemed as though Chuck Whitney might be part of the general conspiracy.

Impulsively, I called him on the intercom. "Did you say our Contact Unit had spoken with C. No just before he attempted suicide?"

"Right. It was Ashton who stopped him. Say, what's this all about?"

"Just an idea. I want you to arrange to drop me into the simulator on a surveillance circuit for a face-to-face with Phil Ashton."

"Won't be possible for a couple of days—not with all this reprograming and reorientation."

I sighed. "Put it on a double shift basis."

I snapped off the IC just as the door swung open to admit Horace P. Siskin, all trim and immaculate in a gray pinstripe and wearing the most cordial smile in his facial repertory.

He came around the desk. "Well, Doug, what did you think of him?"

"Who?"

"Wayne Hartson, of course. Quite a character. The party wouldn't have its foot in the administrative door without him."

"So I heard," I said dryly. "But I didn't quite jump up and click my heels over the privilege of meeting him."

Siskin laughed—a high-pitched but still lusty outburst that left me regarding him quizzically. He commandeered my chair and swiveled around to face the window.

"Don't think much of him myself, son. I doubt he's a good influence on either the party or the country."

That took me by surprise. "And I suppose you're going to do something about it?"

He scanned the ceiling and said intensely, "I rather think I am—with your help, of course."

He aimed a full minute's worth of silence at me. When I didn't react, he went on:

"Hall, I think you're observant enough to know I'm a man of no small ambitions. And I'm proud of my drive and industry. How would you like to see those same qualities applied to the administrative affairs of this country?"

"Under a one-party system?" I asked cautiously.

"One party or ten parties—who gives a damn? What we want is the most capable national leadership available! Can you think of a bigger financial empire than the one I've created? Is there anyone more logically qualified to sit in the White House?"

When his expression questioned my patient smile, I explained, "I can't picture you displacing characters like Hartson."

"Won't be difficult," he assured. "Not with the simulator calling the shots. When we program our electromathematical community on a politically-oriented basis, one Horace P. Siskin is going to be a prominent ID unit. Not an exact replica, perhaps. Maybe we'll brush up on the image a bit."

He paused in reflection. "At any rate, I want it so that when we consult Simulacron-3 for political advice, the Siskin image will assert itself as the ideal candidate type."

I only stared at him. He could do it. I saw that his plan would succeed if only because it was so bold—and logical. Now I was more thankful than ever that I had decided to string along with Reactions so I might be in position to do something about the alliance between Siskin and the party.

Dorothy Ford broke in over the intercom. "There are two men out here from the Association of Reaction Monitors who—"

The door opened as the CRMs, indignant and impatient, ushered themselves in.

"You Hall?" one of them demanded.

When I nodded, the other stormed, "Well, you can tell Siskin—"

"Tell him yourself." I gestured toward the chair.

Siskin swiveled around to face them. "Yes?"

The pair were uniformly surprised.

"We represent ARM," the first said. "And here it is, without trimmings: Either you stop work on this simulator thing or we'll call a walkout by every reaction monitor in the city!"

Siskin started to brush off the threat with a laugh. But instead a grim cast claimed his face. It wasn't difficult to guess why. One-fourth of all employment was accountable, in one way or another, to the opinion polling concerns. And maximum profit for the Establishment depended upon full employment. Siskin, of course, could withstand the assault by falling back on his reserves. But within a week's time there wouldn't be a businessman or housewife who wouldn't be lined up solidly with ARM. Eventual destruction of the Association was, indeed, part of the Establishment's strategy, but not until the financial empire had braced itself for the repercussions.

Not waiting for his answer, the pair strode out.

"Well," I said, somewhat amused, "what do we do now?"

Siskin smiled. "I don't know what you're going to do. But I'm going to find a handful of strings and start pulling them."

Two days later I made myself comfortable on another couch in the peephole department and let Whitney lower a different type of transfer helmet on my head. There was no banter this time, since he had sensed my impatience.

I watched him throw the surveillance circuit switch.

The projection came off smoothly. One second I was reclining on leather upholstery, the next, I was standing in an analog videophone booth. Since it wasn't an empathy coupling, I wasn't imprisoned in the back of some ID unit's mind. Instead, *I was there*—in a pseudo-physical sense.

A tall, thin man stepped out of the next booth. He approached and I could see he was trembling. "Mr. Hall?" he asked uncertainly.

Nodding, I scanned the typical hotel lobby setting. "Is anything wrong?"

"No," he said miserably. "Nothing *you* would appreciate."

"What is it, Ashton?" I reached for his arm but he drew back shuddering.

Then he found words for his distress. "Suppose, in your world, a god dropped down and started talking with you."

I could appreciate his humble, awed perspective. I seized him by the shoulder nevertheless. "Forget it. Right now I'm just like you—a sentient bundle of simulectronic charges."

He turned half away. "Let's get it over with. Then you can go back." He jerked his head in an indefinite direction.

"I didn't realize direct contact would be this difficult."

"What did you expect?" he demanded scornfully. "A picnic?"

"Ashton, we're going to work out something. Maybe we can relieve you of your duty as a Contact Unit."

"Just yank me completely. Wipe me clean. I wouldn't want to go on, knowing what I know."

Ill at ease, I hurried to the point. "I wanted to talk with you about Cau No."

"Lucky, deprogramed devil," he commented.

"You spoke with him just before he tried to kill himself?"

He nodded. "I'd had my eye on him for some time. I sensed he was going to crack up."

I stared intensely into his face. "Phil, it wasn't just the meteors and the storm that set him off, was it?"

He looked up sharply. "How did you know?"

"There *was* something else then?"

"Yes." His shoulders fell. "I didn't say anything about it. I was vindictive, spiteful. I wanted to let Cau No have full rein—wreck the whole damned setup. Then you'd have to wipe everything clean and make a second start."

"What was it that set him off?"

The man hesitated, then blurted it out. "He knew. Somehow he found out what he was, what this whole rotten, make-believe city was. He knew it was only part of a counterfeit world, that his reality was nothing but a reflection of electronic processes."

I sat up stiffly. Whatever information Fuller had consigned to the Cau No entity, it had had that terrific an impact—enough to alert him to the fact that he was merely an analog human being.

"How did he find out?" I asked.

"I wouldn't know."

"Did he talk about anything else, any restricted data that might have been impressed on his drums?"

"No. He was just obsessed with the idea that he was—nothing."

I glanced down at my watch. And I regretted having allotted myself only ten minutes for this face-to-face. "Time's up," I said, heading back for the videophone booth. "I'll drop down and see you again."

"No!" Phil Ashton called after me. "For God's sake, don't!"

I pressed back in the booth, closed the door and watched the second hand of my analog watch creep up on the minute.

With two seconds to go, I glanced out into the lobby. And I almost shouted at what I saw.

Fighting a sickening sense of loss because I knew I couldn't stop retransfer, I watched the familiar figure of Morton Lynch—an *analog* Morton Lynch—crossing the hotel lobby.

⋆SEVEN⋆

I SPENT THE REST OF that afternoon figuratively cowering from the simulator. Now it was something fearful and ominous—an electronic ogre that had breathed purpose into its own soul and had somehow charged into my world to slay Fuller and seize Lynch.

Eventually, it occurred to me that the Morton Lynch I had sighted in the analog hotel lobby might have been a reactional unit who only *resembled* him. It wasn't until the next morning, however, that I realized there was a simple check I could make. With that objective in mind, I hurried to the ID indexing department.

In the "Occupation" file I searched under "Security." No entry. Under the theory that Lynch's simulectronic vocation might be a near equivalent of his real one, I looked under "Police." Still no results.

Then, conceding that I might be suspecting subterfuge where none had been intended, I decided on a more direct approach and crossed over to the nominal files.

The last entry under the L's was: "LYNCH, Morton—IDU-7683."

My hand trembled as I scanned the notations on the card. IDU-7683 had been programed into the simulator three months earlier by Dr. Fuller himself!

Abruptly, curtains parted on indistinct memory and I recalled the incident, made obscure by its insignificance. As a practical joke, Fuller had modeled a unit trait for trait after the real Lynch. Then he had treated the security director to a shocking look-see into the simulator, where Lynch had observed—himself.

I was elated. I had proved, to myself at least, that there had once been a Morton Lynch!

Or *had* there?

Hopelessly, I shrank once again before the reasonable alternative, the redeeming circumstance: Couldn't the entire basis of my belief in Lynch's former existence have been the subconscious knowledge that such a character had been programed into the machine? Had that buried memory festered until I created an imaginary Lynch in real life?

Despondent, I wandered out of the building. I went aimlessly past the row of ARM pickets, remaining on the staticstrip where I could feel the reassuring solidity of concrete beneath my feet. I just wanted to walk until I ran out of the city and lost myself in silent, desolate fields. But then I thought of my last venture into the country and banished both the memory and the wishful intent.

At the corner a pollster stopped me. "I'm sampling reaction to fall styles in men's clothing," he announced.

I only stared through him.

"Do you approve of the broad lapel?" he began.

But when he reached for his pad I stumbled on down the street.

"Hey, come back!" he shouted. "I'll have you fined!"

Under the pedistrip overpass at the corner an automatic news vendor blared: "Reaction Monitors in Trouble! Legislation Offered to Ban Public Polling!"

Even that—even the fact that Siskin had already started pulling his strings against ARM—made no impression on me.

While I stood there another pollster drew up before me. Softly, out of the side of his mouth, he said, "For God's sake—for your own sake, Hall—forget about the whole damned thing!"

Jolted by the naked pertinence of the warning, I made a stab for his arm but came up with only his CRM sleeve band as he whirled and disappeared into the throng.

It *hadn't* happened, I told myself numbly. I'd only *imagined* the presence of the pollster. But my lack of conviction was understandable as I stuffed his cloth badge into my pocket.

An air car detached itself from the swift, smooth traffic flow and pulled up at the curb.

"Doug!" Jinx called out cheerfully. "I was just going to see if you'd have lunch with me."

Then she discovered the blankness on my face. "Get in, Doug."

Submissively, I climbed into the car and she maneuvered onto a liftoff island. In a moment we were soaring up.

We roofed out through the highest regulated level and she adjusted the autosystem for drift compensation. We sat there, high above the city.

"Now," she said tentatively, "what's the trouble? Have a run-in with Siskin?"

She cracked open the dome and a sighing penetration of refreshing wind wafted the cobwebs from my entangled thoughts. But they were thoughts that were still too inchoate to wrestle with imponderables.

"Doug?" She questioned my silence as the draft caught a tress of lustrous hair and splayed it against the plexidome.

If I was certain of anything, it was that the time was past for intrigue. I had to know whether she had actually been devious with me or whether I had only imagined that too.

"Jinx," I asked her outright, "what are you hiding?"

She glanced away. And my suspicions were strengthened.

"I've got to know!" I exclaimed. "Something's happening to me. God, I don't want you to be involved too!"

Her eyes moistened and her lips trembled imperceptibly.

"All right," I went on stubbornly. "I'll come to the point. Your father was murdered because of some secret information he had. The only man who knew anything about it has disappeared. Two attempts were made on my life. I watched a road vanish. A pollster I never saw before just walked up and told me to forget about it."

She began crying openly. But I felt no sympathy. Everything I had said had meant something to her. I was sure of that. Now she had only to admit that, somehow, she too was part of the picture.

"Oh, Doug," she pleaded. "Can't you just *forget* about it?"

Wasn't that what the reaction monitor had just proposed?

"Don't you see you can't go on like that?" she begged. "Don't you realize what you're doing to yourself?"

What *I* was doing to *myself*?

Then I understood. She hadn't been hiding *anything*! All along, what I had interpreted as duplicity had actually been compassion. She had only been trying to steer me calmly away from my unreasonable suspicions, my obsessions!

She had sensed my irrational behavior. Perhaps Collingsworth had told her about the incident at Limpy's. And her deep solicitude had been founded on a structure of crumbling dreams. She had nurtured her childhood "crush" through adolescence and into maturity, only to find fulfillment blocked by what she must have imagined was mental instability.

"I'm sorry, Doug," she said hopelessly. "I'll take you down."

There wasn't anything I could say.

I spent the afternoon at Limpy's, smoking enough cigarettes to leave my mouth tasting like a burnt rag but cooling it off more than occasionally with a Scotch-asteroid.

At sundown I started walking purposelessly through the almost deserted heart of the city. Eventually I moved onto the automatic sidewalk and wound up on an express strip whose destination I hadn't even noticed.

At length the chill of night revived me to a vague awareness of where my indefinite flight had been taking me. As I reached the terminal platform, I glanced up to find myself in a residential section not too far from Avery Collingsworth's home. What better destination, under the circumstances, than a psychological consultant?

Naturally, Avery was surprised.

"Say, where have you been?" He ushered me in. "I looked for you all afternoon to get your okay on another batch of reactional units."

"I had some business outside the office."

Of course, he had noticed my haggard appearance. But, tactfully, he said nothing.

Collingsworth's home bore profuse evidence of his status as a bachelor. His study had apparently not been straightened out in weeks. But somehow I felt at ease confronted by the disarray of books, his cluttered desk and a floor strewn with crumpled paper.

"Drink?" he invited, after I had sunk into a chair.

"Scotch. Straight."

The order came promptly out of his autotender and he brought it over. Smiling, he ran a hand through his silken white hair. "Along with this goes the offer of a shave and a fresh shirt."

I grinned and downed the drink.

He drew up a chair. "You can tell me about it now."

"It won't be easy."

"Zeno? Someone named Morton Lynch? That sort of stuff?"

I nodded.

"I'm glad you came, Doug. Damned glad. There's more than just the sketch and Lynch, isn't there?"

"A lot more. But I don't quite know how to get into it."

He leaned back. "I remember a week or so ago in Limpy's I said something about mixing psychology with simulectronics and getting a lot of oddball convictions. Let me quote myself: 'You can hardly stuff people into machines without starting to wonder about the basic nature of both.' Suppose you take it from there."

I did. I told him everything. And throughout the account his expression didn't change. When I had finished, he rose and paced.

"First," he offered, "don't try any self-depreciation. Look at it objectively. Fuller had his troubles too. Oh, not as developed as yours. But then, he didn't take the simulator to as advanced a stage as you have."

"What are you trying to say?"

"That the type of work you're doing can't be pursued without unavoidable psychological consequences."

"I don't understand."

"Doug, you're a god. You have omnipotent control over an entire city of pseudo people—an analog world. Sometimes you have to take actions that don't square with your moral convictions, like wiping off an ID entity. Results? Pangs of conscience. So, in essence, what do we have? Ups and downs. Phases of lofty exhilaration, followed by descent into the depths of self-incrimination. You ever experience that type of reaction?"

"Yes." I realized only then that I had.

"And do you know what condition I've just described?"

I nodded and whispered, "Paranoia."

He laughed quickly. "But just a false paranoia—an *induced* condition. Oh, it's a valid, convincing thing. Has all the earmarks too: delusions of grandeur, loss of contact, suspicions of persecution, hallucinations." He paused. Then, even more sincerely: "Don't you see what's happening? You wipe off an analog reactional unit and you fancy someone in your own world vanishing. You reprogram the past experiences of a counterfeit population and you think your own background is being tampered with."

Even confused as I was, I could appreciate the logic in his explanation. "Let's suppose you're right. What do I do about it?"

"You've already done ninety per cent of what has to be done. The most important things are realization and self-confrontation." He rose suddenly. "Dial yourself another drink while I make a videocall."

When he returned I had not only finished the drink, but was also half through shaving in the bathroom adjoining the study.

"That's the spirit!" he encouraged. "I'll get the shirt."

But when he came back I was frowning again. "What about those blackouts? *They* are real, at least."

"Oh, I'm sure they are, in a psychosomatic sense. Your integrity revolts against the idea of psychosis. So you look for a face-saving excuse. Blackouts put the whole thing on an organic plane. You don't feel so humiliated."

When I had finished dressing he led me to the door and suggested, "Make good use of that shirt."

His advice was meaningless until I found Dorothy Ford parked in front of the house. Then even the purpose behind his videocall became clear. Good ol' Dorothy—all too ready to give me the "lift" Collingsworth had apparently suggested I needed. Whether she was disposed to run a mercy mission made no difference. Here was an opportunity to keep her eye on one of Siskin's assets.

But I didn't mind.

We speared into the silent blackness and sat suspended between a panoply of cold stars and the brilliant carpet of city lights. Against the graceful curve of the plexidome, Dorothy was a warm, soft picture, full of vitality and eagerness. Her hair, fluorescing with the reflected glow of the instrument panel, was a flaxen backdrop for a smile both vivid and anxious.

"Well," she said, elevating flawlessly rounded shoulders, "shall I submit a plan of action? Or do you have ideas of your own?"

"Collingsworth call you into the picture?"

She nodded. "Thought you needed a bracer." Then she laughed. "And I'm just the gal who can give it to you."

"Sounds like interesting therapy."

"Oh, but it is!" Her eyes glistened with mock suggestiveness.

Then, suddenly, she was serious. "Doug, we both have our jobs. It's more than obvious mine is to see that you stay tucked safely in the Great Little One's pocket. But there's no reason why we can't have fun at the same time. Agreed?"

"Agreed." I accepted her hand. "So what's on the program?"

"How about something—for real?"

"Like what?" I asked cautiously.

"A shot or two of cortical current."

I smiled tolerantly at her.

"Well don't look so damned reserved," she quipped. "It's not illegal, you know."

"I didn't figure you for the type who might need an ESB fix."

"I don't." She reached over and patted my hand. "But, darling, Dr. Collingsworth says *you* do."

The Cortical Corner was a modest, one-story building nestling between two soaring obelisks of concrete and glass on the northern fringe of the downtown section. Outside, impulsive and boisterous teen-agers jostled one another, surging occasionally against their parked air jalopies and spilling frequently into the almost abandoned traffic lanes. Eventually, they would pool their resources and finance a cortical-kicks session for a select member of the group.

Inside, in the waiting lounge, clients sat around with patient politeness, listening to the music or sipping drinks. They were mostly elderly women, uncomfortable in their embarrassment but none the less eager. Few, including the men, were below their mid-thirties. Which attested to the fact that the youthful adult group generally didn't require ESB escapism.

We waited only long enough for Dorothy to inform the hostess that we were interested in the triply-expensive tandem circuit.

Without delay we were admitted to a luxuriously appointed alcove. Omniphonic music susurrated against period tapestries. Poignant scents hung heavy in the warm air.

We settled down onto the velvet couch and Dorothy nestled snugly beneath my arm, her cheek upon my chest and the fragrance of her perfumed hair rising into my face. The attendant lowered the headpieces and swung the control panel to within Dorothy's reach.

"Just relax and leave it to little Dottie," she said, squirming to grip the selectors.

Tingling current lanced instantly from scores of electrodes, sensing and homing in on appropriate cortical centers. The room, the tapestries, the scents—all were swept away like thistledown scattered by a gale.

Delicate azure skies stretched overhead, blanketing a lazy-rolling, emerald sea that washed with soothing monotony upon a beach of purest sand. Surging water buoyed me up, then dropped me again in a sluggish, wavering motion until my toes touched the rippled bottom.

It wasn't an illusion. It was *real*. There was no doubting the validity of the experience, even though it sprang solely from excited hallucination centers. Cortical stimulation was *that* effective.

There was a tinkle of laughter behind me and, on the crest of the next swell, I treaded around, only to intercept a faceful of splashed water.

Dorothy shoved off, out of my reach. I went after her and she crash-dived, exposing in glistening, fleeting array the sun-washed bareness of her firm, supple body.

We swam under water and once I even drew close enough to seize her by the ankle before she wrenched free and was off again, like a graceful creature of the sea.

I broke surface and spewed out a mouthful of brine.

And there was Jinx Fuller, standing on the beach, tense and concerned as she scanned the frothing seascape. The wind whipped her skirt and tossed her hair about her face.

Dorothy surfaced, saw Jinx and scowled. "It's no good here."

Blackness swept across the warp of my senses, then Dorothy and I were on skis, flashing down the frozen, white breast of a mountain and laughing against the chill spray of powdered snow.

We slowed and tried a shallow curve around an irregular rise. She took a spill and I braked, returning to drop down beside her.

She laughed heartily, slipped her goggles up onto her forehead and caught my neck within her arms.

But I only stared beyond her—at Jinx. Half concealed by an ice-tinseled tree, she was a silent, pensive witness.

And in that preoccupied moment I sensed it—the gentle, furtive presence of Dorothy Ford's questing thoughts, boring, together with the excitative currents, into layer after layer of cortical tissue.

I had forgotten about the resonant effects of a reciprocating ESB circuit; forgotten that coupled stimulation could bring about an involuntary surrender of thoughts by one of the subjects.

I reared erect on the couch and snapped off my headpiece.

Dorothy, coming up with me, offered an indifferent shrug. Then she gave new meaning to an age-old feminine quip: "Can't blame a girl for trying, can you?"

I only scanned her face for information. Had she gone deep enough to learn that I was staying on with Siskin only because I intended to sabotage his conspiracy with the party?

✴EIGHT✴

FOR THE FIRST TIME IN weeks I was finally out from under the pall of Fuller's death. And the imagined incidents that had followed in the wake of that accident were like a nightmare losing its vivid focus in the fresh, wholesome light of dawn. I had come back from a terrifying brink, thanks to Avery Collingsworth.

Pseudoparanoia. It was so logical that I wondered why it had never occurred to either Fuller or myself that involvement with the total environment simulator and its too-real "little people" would pose unanticipated mental hazards.

There were still complications to be unraveled, of course. Dorothy Ford, for instance, had to understand that our escapade in the ESB den had meant nothing to me. Although I had enjoyed the swim, so to speak, I wasn't going to make a habit of it. Not after the cortical excitation experiences had so clearly demonstrated my preoccupation with Jinx Fuller.

Dorothy had gathered as much, though. I found that out the next morning when I paused in front of her desk.

"About last night, Doug—" she offered distantly. "As I said, we both have our jobs. And I've got to do mine loyally. I have no choice."

I wondered what sort of sword Siskin held over her. Mine had two edges—the threats of an accelerated police investigation into Fuller's death, with me as the goat, and of his finally *not* deciding to let the simulator be used partly for sociological research.

"Now that we know the score," Dorothy added less formally, "there won't be any misunderstanding." She softened further, touching my hand. "And, Doug, it can still be fun."

I remained aloof, though, not knowing how much she had picked from my inner thoughts through the ESB hookup.

Anxiety over the possibility that she had learned and told Siskin of my intentions found full cause for amplification two days later. That was when he summoned me to the Inner Establishment.

The air limousine cushioned down on a landing shelf outside the one hundred and thirty-third level of the Establishment's Babel Central. Siskin himself was waiting at the entrance to his office.

He hooked his hand over my shoulder and walked me across cloud-like Syrterene carpeting. Beside his acre-large, gold-trimmed desk, he paused and stared out through the vast window. Far below, the city was like a distant, fuzzy painting, obscured by haze and half hidden by drifting puffs of cotton.

Abruptly he said, "Something's gone wrong with our legislation against the reaction monitors. It was tabled. There won't be any action this session."

I held back an amused smile over Siskin's discomfiture. It was only the threat of having opinion sampling outlawed as a public nuisance that had blunted the ARM offensive against Reactions. "Apparently the monitors have more power than you figured them for."

"But it doesn't make sense. Hartson assured me he had the entire committee in his vest pocket."

I shrugged. "Well, there goes your lever. Nothing will keep the pollsters from striking now."

"I wouldn't bet on that." Suddenly he was grinning. "How articulate are you on the idea of using Simulacron-3 for carving out the millennium in human relations?"

Puzzled, I said, "I have my convictions. But I don't suppose I'm prepared to deliver a speech on them."

"And that's *exactly* how I prefer it. That way the sincerity will show through."

He spoke sharply into the intercom: "Send them in."

They came in—a score of wirephotographers and reporters, network cameramen, roving commentators. They gathered around the desk, pinning us in a tight semicircle.

Siskin held up his hands for silence.

"As you know," he said, "Reactions is feeling the pressure of organized coercion at the hands of the Association of Reaction Monitors. They will call a strike and bring down economic chaos, they tell us, unless we close shop and deprive the country of the greatest social advance of the age."

He climbed upon a chair and shouted against the ripple of skeptical voices:

"All right—I know what you're thinking: that this is a promotional stunt. Well, it isn't! I'm fighting to save our simulator—*your* simulator—because it isn't merely a money-making venture. It's also the instrument that's going to carve out a *bright, new future for the human race!* It's going to lift man a mile high from the primeval slime in which he has wallowed since his dawn!"

He let that much sink in, then said: "I'm going to have the driving force behind the total environment simulator give you the details himself—Douglas Hall."

Siskin's strategy was not obscure. If he could make the public believe his simulectronic marvel was going to mass-produce glimmering halos for the human race, then no force would be able to stand against REIN—not even the reaction monitors.

I faced the cameras uneasily. "The simulator offers vast opportunity for research in the field of human relations. That opportunity was uppermost in Dr. Fuller's mind."

I paused, suddenly aware of something that hadn't occurred to me before: If public sentiment could beat down the ARM offensive, then it might also insure exclusive use of the system *for improving human relations!* The people would rise up in wrath against the Establishment whenever I decided to tell them Siskin's machine would serve only political and personal ambitions!

Eagerly, I pushed on. "We have here a surgical instrument that can dissect the very soul itself! It can take a human being apart, motive by motive, instinct by instinct. It can dig to the core of our basic drives, fears, aspirations. It can track down and study, analyze, classify and *show us how to do something about* every trait that goes into the makeup of any individual. It can explain and uncover the sources of prejudice, bigotry, hate, perverse sentiment. By studying analog beings in a simulated system, we can chart the entire spectrum of human relations. By prodding those analog units, we can observe not only the beginning, but also *every step* in the development of undesirable, antisocial tendencies!"

Siskin stepped forward. "You can see, gentlemen, that Mr. Hall is somewhat of a fanatic on his subject. But the Siskin Establishment would have it no other way."

I picked it up again. "In the conditioned environment of Simulacron-3, we expect to isolate various reactional units, from analog children on up through every age group. Systematically, we'll nudge them first one way and then the other with every conceivable stimulus that will bring out the best and worst in them. We expect to advance the study of human behavior by thousands of years."

What I was saying wasn't original. I was only repeating phrases Fuller had tossed at me with boundless enthusiasm over the years. And I could but hope I was getting them across with a sincerity equal to his own.

"The simulator," I summed up, "will point the way to the Golden Age in human relations. It will show us how to cleanse the mortal spirit of the last vestiges of its animal origins."

Siskin took over. "Before you start firing your questions, I want to clear up some of the less glamorous details. First, our Establishment went into this thing with the idea of making a profit. However, I have long since rejected that incentive. Now I want to devote all this organization's energy to seeing that the wonderful things expected of Mr. Hall's simulator are realized."

I let him commit himself. When the time came, I would have only to let word of the Siskin-party conspiracy leak out.

"Reactions," he said gravely, "is going to have a commercial function too. As much as I regret it, that's the way it has to be. Oh, we could apply for government grants instead. But, gentlemen, you have to realize that this new, great Foundation can be beholden to *no one*. It must operate above all levels."

One of the newsmen asked, "What do you mean by 'commercial functions'?"

"Simply that the simulator will have to earn the considerable funds needed to carry out its humanitarian purpose. Reactions *will* accept commercial, behavior-forecasting contracts. But only a bare minimum of them. Only as many as will be necessary to make up the operational deficit that will recur annually, even after I endow the Foundation immediately with an additional two hundred and fifty million."

That went over big with the press corps. And it tightened the noose even more securely around the Lilliputian Siskin neck.

We spent the next half hour fielding questions. It was apparent, though, that we had left no room for skepticism. After the newsmen left, Siskin did a fairylike dance and ended up embracing me.

"You put on a good show, son—a great show!" he exclaimed. "I couldn't have done half as well!"

By the next day floodgates had opened to loose a surging tide of public opinion on the Siskin announcement. Among all the stories and videocasts, the human interest columns and editorial expressions, there was not an unfavorable word. Never before had I seen anything capture the general imagination as had Siskin's "great humanitarian effort."

Before noon, commendatory resolutions had been passed by the City Council and the State House of Representatives. On the national level, a concurrent Congressional measure was being drafted.

With the suddenness of an avalanche, new organizations were proposed as allies of the "noble endeavor." Two mass meetings that evening drew out separate groups of enthusiasts who decided on the lofty names "Simulectronic Samaritans, Inc.," and "Tomorrow—the Whole Human." I suppose it would have been difficult to find anyone who wasn't afire with idealism. The hoodwinking had been that complete.

Sensing the buildup of public support for REIN, the Association of Reaction Monitors prudently reduced the number of their pickets to a mere ten. But even then the police riot squad was reinforced to protect them from scores of irate Siskin sympathizers.

As for myself, I was riding a crest of elation, having climbed up out of the depths of self-doubt. Not only had my personal problems evaporated, thanks to Collingsworth's counsel, but triumph over Siskin and the party seemed inevitable.

Smugly armed with the well-publicized evidence of my return to normalcy, I videoed Jinx the next afternoon for a dinner date. Although she seemed somewhat unimpressed with the humanitarian course Siskin had charted for Reactions, she promptly accepted my invitation. But I was left uncomfortable with the notion that she had been reluctant.

Determined to insure a proper start for a change, I brought her to John's Late Sixties—exclusive, expensive, and fairly exuding an atmosphere that had been, as the ads had put it, "left untouched for over two generations."

The sharp scent of food (natural edibles, not the synthetic stuff) under preparation in the adjoining kitchen eventually captured Jinx's fancy. And, while we waited to eat, she gradually warmed up to the harmonies of antiquity that were all around us—the bluntly functional chairs and tables, the latter quaint with their "cloth" coverings; incandescent bulbs; a string ensemble that was doing a valiant job, I suppose, with its rock 'n' roll selections.

A waitress who came to ask what we wanted and later returned with the order was the crowning anachronism that brought Jinx around to full appreciation of the place.

"I think this is a fascinating idea!" she exclaimed over her salad of actual, green vegetables.

"Good. Then there's no reason why we shouldn't repeat it."

"No. I don't suppose there is."

Had I detected perhaps a trace of restraint? Was it that she was still wary of me?

I took her hand. "Ever hear of pseudoparanoia?"

Puzzlement deprived her brow of some of its smoothness.

"I hadn't either," I went on, "until I spoke with Collingsworth. He explained that what I was experiencing was only the psychological effects of working with the simulator. What I'm trying to say, Jinx, is that I was off balance until a couple of days ago. But I'm squared away now."

Her features, though alert, were somehow rigid in abstraction—soft and gentle, beautiful, yet at the same time cold and distant.

"I'm glad everything's all right," she said simply.

Somehow it wasn't turning out quite as I had planned.

We were silent throughout most of the main course. Finally I decided I would put up with my hesitancy no longer.

I leaned across the table. "Collingsworth said that whatever upset me was just temporary."

"I'm sure he was right." Only her words were dull and heavy.

I reached for her hand. But she slid it tactfully out of range.

Discouraged, I said, "The night we took that ride—remember? You asked me what I wanted to find in life."

She nodded, but only perfunctorily.

"This isn't coming off as well as I thought it would," I complained.

She sat there staring at me, indecision playing across her obviously troubled face.

Bewildered, I asked, "Didn't you say something about having never stopped thinking of me?"

"Oh, Doug. Let's not talk about it. Not now."

"*Why* not now?"

She didn't answer.

At first I had thought she was running from something vast and mysterious. Then I had imagined it was only I whom she feared. Now I didn't know *what* to think.

She indicated her supposedly shiny nose, excused herself and headed across the floor, elegant in the rhythm of her motions and attracting admiring glances all the way.

Then my hands contracted into fists and I slumped forward. I sat there through long minutes, trembling, trying to pull back from the brink of a yawning blackness. The room wavered and faded and a thousand rivers of fire coursed through my head.

"Doug! Are you all right?"

Jinx's solicitous voice, the touch of her hand on my shoulder brought me swimming back.

"It's nothing," I lied. "Just a headache."

But as I went for her wrap, I wondered about Collingsworth's assurance that the lapses had been only psychosomatic. Perhaps there was a lingering effect here that might be expected to continue for a while, even after the rest of the trouble had cleared.

My confusion only contributed to the silence between us as I cushioned Jinx home. At her door, I caught her arms and pulled her close. But she only turned her face aside. It was as though she had devoted the entire evening to but one purpose—discouraging me.

I headed back for the door.

Then, crowning her inconsistency, she called out in a small, uncertain voice, "I will see you again, won't I, Doug?"

When I finally turned around, however, she had already gone in.

I couldn't let the evening end on this completely irrational note. There was only one thing to do—go back and insist on her explaining why she had been so distant.

Striding ahead, I reached for the buzzer. Before I could touch it, though, the door swung open. I had forgotten that Dr. Fuller had keyed it to my capacitance.

I stood on the threshold. "Jinx."

There was no answer.

I went through the living room and dining room and into the study. "Jinx?"

I checked the other rooms, then went through the entire house once more, looking behind doors, in closets, under beds.

"Jinx! Jinx!"

I sprinted to the back door and felt its servo unit. Cold. It hadn't been opened in the last half hour, at least.

But Jinx was gone. It was as though I had only imagined seeing her enter the house.

✭ⴖⵊⴖᴇ✭

AGAIN THE EQUALLY UNTENABLE ALTERNATIVES. Either Collingsworth was wrong in his conviction that cure of pseudoparanoia lay merely in its recognition. Or Jinx Fuller *had* vanished.

Hours after my frantic search of her home, I parked the car in the garage, then lingered irresolutely in the sulking shadows outside my apartment building. Without even realizing I had stepped onto the low-speed pedistrip, I soon found myself belting through quiet, desolate sections of the city.

Inadequately, I tried to cope with my dilemma. There *had* been disappearances. Jinx's had proved that much. And that same impossible fate *had* befallen Morton Lynch, a sketch of Achilles and the tortoise, a trophy plaque bearing Lynch's name, a stretch of road together with the countryside through which it ran.

With Lynch and the drawing, it was still as though they had never existed. The road and the countryside had returned. What about Jinx? Would she be back—leaving me to wonder whether I had actually searched her house and failed to find her? Or would I soon begin learning that nobody else had ever heard of her?

During early morning I left the pedistrip twice to call Jinx's home. But each time there was no answer.

Gliding again through deserted downtown sections, I could almost feel the dreadful presence of an Unknown Force closing in on me—a determined, malevolent Agency that lurked behind every shadow.

Before dawn I had phoned three more times. And each futile call drove home the awful suspicion that I would never hear of her again. But why? Lynch's disappearance was logical. He had been acting in defiance of the Unknown Force. Jinx, on the other hand, had insisted her father's death was an accident.

Yet now she was gone.

Shortly after sunrise, I had coffee at an automat, then belted unhurriedly to Reactions. There I found an apprehensive group of ARM pickets huddling on the staticstrip and protected by riot squad members from scores of angry Siskin supporters.

Someone raised a length of pipe to hurl it at the reaction monitors. But one of the officers leveled his laser gun. A cone of crimson light stabbed out and the man collapsed, temporarily paralyzed. The demonstrators retreated.

In my office I spent the next hour wearing a path around the desk. Eventually, Dorothy Ford came in, drew back in surprise on seeing me there so early, then continued on over to the closet.

"I'm having a hard time keeping tabs on you," she said, delicately removing a small, pointed hat without disturbing the pageboy. "And that's bad because the Great Little One probably figures that by now we ought to be nesting together."

She studded the closet door closed. "I tried to reach you during the night. You weren't home."

"I ..."

"No explanations necessary. I wasn't looking for you for myself. Siskin just wanted to make certain you'd be down early this morning."

"I'm down early," I said flatly. "What's on his mind?"

"He doesn't confide *everything* in me." She headed back toward the reception room, but paused. "Doug, was it that Fuller girl?"

Facing the window at the moment, I spun around. The very mention of Jinx's name had had that effect. It had assured me that, thus far at least, Jinx wasn't following in Lynch's footsteps. As yet, the evidences of her existence weren't being obliterated.

Before I could answer, Siskin swept into the office, frowned up at me, and exclaimed, "You look like you spent the night ESB-ing!"

Then he saw Dorothy and his expression softened. He stared back and forth between us. For me, his gaze, beneath slightly raised eyebrows, was calculative. For her, it was one of subtle approbation, not without its sensual implications—a tactful pat on the back for services effectively rendered.

Crossing behind him, she shrugged and cast me a there-you-see-what-*he*-thinks glance.

As she studded the door open he called after her, "I left a gentleman in the reception room. Will you show him in?"

"Another party man?" I asked.

"No. Someone in *your* line of work. You'll recognize him."

I did. It was Marcus Heath. He was short, though not nearly as diminutive as Siskin. Stout, but not solidly packed. Thick-lensed glasses only magnified the restlessness in his gray eyes.

"Hello, Hall," he said. "It's been some time, hasn't it?"

It had at that. I hadn't seen him since the trouble at the university. But it wasn't likely he had spent the entire ten years in prison. Then I remembered his sentence had been for only two years.

"Heath will be your assistant," Siskin explained. "But we're going to give him the run of the place."

I laced the man with a critical stare. "Have you been keeping up with developments in simulectronics?"

"I've stayed a step ahead of them, Hall. I've been in charge of technical work for Barnfeld."

"I bought him off," Siskin boasted. "Now he's with us."

Barnfeld was the only other private organization that had been rivaling Reactions in simulectronics research.

I leaned back against the desk. "Heath, does Mr. Siskin know all about you?"

"About that thing at the university?" Siskin interrupted. "Of course I do. Enough to realize Heath was the goat."

"Dr. Heath," I reminded him, "was convicted of fraud in the misuse of public research funds."

"You didn't *believe* that, did you, Doug?" Heath pleaded.

"You confessed to it."

Siskin stepped between us. "I'm not stupid enough to hire a man without fully investigating his background. I turned my entire staff loose on it. Heath was covering up for—somebody else."

"That's a lie!" I protested. "Fuller didn't have a penny when he left the University."

Siskin's tiny white teeth showed. "I said I was satisfied with Heath's credentials. That's all that's necessary."

With that, he led the man out. At the same moment I realized the reason behind this latest maneuver. Dorothy Ford *had* tapped in telepathically, over the tandem ESB circuit, on my intentions to sabotage the Siskin-party tie-up and block his political ambitions.

And now Siskin was preparing to get along without me. Heath would be expected to learn as much as he could. Then the necessary strings would be pulled and I would be arrested for Fuller's murder.

Late that morning the IC buzzer sounded and an elderly, stout-faced woman's image flared on the screen. Dorothy had evidently left her desk and had switched incoming calls onto the direct circuit.

"CRM 10421-C," the woman began. "I'm sampling opinion on—"

"I'll take the fine," I broke in rudely, switching her out.

The buzzer went off again and I flipped the intercom back on. "I said I'd—*Jinx!*"

"Morning, Doug," she greeted, the orderly setting of Dr. Fuller's study visible in the background. "I had to call. I know I acted so—peculiar last night."

"Jinx! What happened? Where did you go? How—?"

Her brow furrowed with puzzlement. Or was it fear?

"I went into the house right after you did," I recounted. "You weren't there. I couldn't find you anywhere!"

She smiled. "You should have looked more closely. I was exhausted. I threw myself across the couch and that was that."

"But I *looked* there!"

"Of course you're mistaken." She dismissed the matter with a laugh. "As for last night: I *was* worried about you. But I'm not now. Not after thinking it over. You see, I had waited so long. And, over the past few days, I had been so disappointed."

I sat back and stared through the screen.

"What I'm trying to say," she added, "is that I *do* love you."

After a moment she asked, "I'll see you this evening?"

"I'm going to be working late," I lied.

"Then I'll pick you up at the office."

"But—"

"Don't argue. I'll wait there all night if I have to."

I didn't argue. I broke the connection, trying desperately to apply reason to what had just happened. She would have me believe she was prepared, last night, never to see me again because she was afraid of me. But now she was ready to accept me, despite the fact I had just given her even *more* reason for concern over my condition!

On the other hand, if she had actually vanished, where had she gone? What had she done during those twelve hours?

Moreover, it was apparent she *hadn't* been running from anything. For if It had overtaken her, only to lose Its grip on her, she wouldn't be acting now as though nothing had happened.

That afternoon I spent half an hour staring down into a cold cup of coffee in the REIN automat and trying to reconcile myself to the idea that Jinx's disappearance *had* been only another hallucination.

"Looks like some awfully profound cogitation."

Starting, I glanced up at Chuck Whitney, realizing he had been standing there for some time. "Just routine problems," I managed.

"I've got this guy Heath in my department. Can't shake him."

"Don't try. You'd be bucking Siskin. But if he gets in your way, let me know."

"I'm letting you know now. I'm just getting ready to hit the couch for an empathy coupling with our Contact Unit. Heath wants a front row seat so he can see how I do it."

"Then I suppose you'll have to give him one."

Puzzled, he asked, "You want me to fill him in on how the system works?"

"Volunteer nothing. But I don't see how we can avoid answering his questions. Why the empathy check on Ashton?"

"Thought I'd see if he's still as bitter as he was."

Ten minutes later I was back at my desk. Staring absently at the blotter, I picked up a pen and let my hand fall mechanically into the motions of recreating Fuller's sketch of Achilles and the tortoise.

Eventually I let the pen slip from my fingers and studied the crude product of my inartistic effort. That the name "Zeno" had been meant to suggest "C. No" was more than obvious. Especially since Cau No had been wiped just before I could reach him.

Zeno's Paradox represented, fundamentally, the proposition that all motion is illusive. And it hadn't taken me long to recognize that all motion *is* illusive—in a counterfeit simulectronic system.

Had the drawing contained possibly *another* concealed meaning? There was Achilles, a hundred feet from the turtle, both in motion. But by the time the Greek ran that hundred feet, the tortoise would have moved ahead, say, ten feet. While Achilles covered, in his turn, that ten feet, his competitor would have pushed on an additional foot. The runner would negotiate that one-foot distance, only to find that the turtle had, meanwhile, inched ahead another tenth of a foot. And so on, *ad infinitum*.

Achilles could never overtake the tortoise.

Had Fuller's sketch been intended to suggest a reduction into the infinite? Then something Fuller had said months earlier swam up in my memory:

"Wouldn't it be interesting if one of our ID units suddenly decided to start building a total environment simulator?"

The side door swung open and hit its stop with a thud. I turned to see who had studded it with such force.

Whitney stood poised on the threshold, gulping air, glancing desperately back down the hallway.

"Chuck!" I exclaimed. "What happened?"

He started at the sound of my voice and cringed against the wall. Then, in an obviously supreme effort to compose himself, he slowed his breathing and steadied his eyes.

"Nothing, Mr. Hall." He sidled toward the reception room door.

But Whitney had *never* called me "Mr. Hall."

I took a step toward him and terror flared in his eyes as he burst for the door. Lunging, I got there first. He swore and swung at me, but I ducked under the hook. I seized his wrist and twisted the arm behind him.

"Let me go!" he shouted frantically.

It all became instantly clear.

"You're *Phil Ashton*!" I whispered.

"Yes." He sagged. "I almost made it. God, *I almost made it!*"

He wrenched free and came at me again, punching, clawing. I swung back with all I had. Then I picked him off the floor and carried his limp form over to the couch.

At the desk, I buzzed the peephole department on the intercom.

One of Whitney's assistants came into focus, the recently used couch and empathy helmet visible in the background. "Yes, Mr. Hall?"

"Anything go wrong in there?"

He paused thoughtfully. "No, sir. Why?"

"Mr. Whitney around?" I glanced at Chuck—the *physical* Chuck, that is—still unconscious on the couch.

"No. But he just finished an empathy coupling with Ashton."

"How did he act when he came out of it?"

"All right, I guess." Then, "Say, he didn't tape his report!"

"Anything else unusual happen?"

He looked confused. "We *did* have a little trouble with Heath. Tried to put in his two cents' worth at the modulator panel."

"He put in more than two cents' worth. He monkeyed with the gain control and gave us a reciprocal transfer. I've got Ashton in my office. Whitney's trapped down there in the simulator. Pick up a couple of the boys and get over here—quick!"

I stood over Ashton, studying Whitney's limp features, hoping fervently that the retransfer process would work. There had been a cataclysmic upheaval of molecular structures in Whitney's brain cells. Patterns etched there over a lifetime had been swept away, re-established among the memory drums and tapes of the Contact Unit's subjective circuits. At the same time, all the data from Ashton's circuits had surged into Whitney's brain cells.

Only successful reversal of the process would bring Chuck back.

Ashton stirred and opened his—Whitney's, that is—eyes.

"I almost made it," he sobbed. "I almost took the *first* step."

He rose shakily. "You can't send me back down there!"

I seized his shoulders and steadied him. "It's going to be all right, Phil. We're going to do away with the Contact Unit system. We'll reorient you. You won't even know your world isn't real."

"Oh, God!" he cried. "I don't want it that way! I don't want *not* to know! But I don't want to *know* either!"

I forced him back onto the couch. But he sprang up again.

"Up here," he shouted, "I'm a step closer to the *real* reality! You've got to let me go on and find the material world!"

"What do you mean?" I asked, trying to humor him. If I didn't steer him carefully through this experience, he might go completely irrational and have to be wiped out of the simulator.

He laughed hysterically. "You utter, damned fool! You're worse off than I am. I *know* what the score is. You don't!"

I shook him. "Snap out of it, Ashton!"

"No. *You're* the one who has to snap out of it! *You're* the one who has to wake up out of your complacent little dream of reality! I lied. I *did* talk with Cau No before you wiped him out of the system. But I didn't say anything because I was afraid you might go berserk and destroy your simulator."

I tensed. "What did No say?"

"You don't know how he found out his world was only a counterfeit, do you?" Ashton was laughing in fanatical triumph. "It was because your Dr. Fuller *told* him. Oh, not directly. He only planted the data in Cau No's subconscious, where he hoped you'd find it. But it didn't stay on No's secondary drums. It leaked out. And No applied the information to his own world."

"What information?" I demanded, shaking him again.

"That *your world too* doesn't exist! *It's just a complex of variable charges in a simulator—nothing more than a reflection of a greater simulectronic process!*"

He sobbed and laughed and I only stood there paralyzed.

"Nothing! Nothing!" he raved. "We're nothing, you and I. Only triumphs of electronic wizardry, simulectronic shadows!"

Then he was on his feet again. "Don't send me back down there! Let's work together. Maybe we'll eventually break through into the bottom of absolute reality! *I* came one step up, didn't I?"

I slugged him again. Not because he was uncontrollable. Only because of the abject mockery of what he had said. Then, as my eyes bored unseeing through the still form of Chuck Whitney on the carpet, a calm sense of reason shouted within me that it was true.

Everything was exactly as Ashton had represented it.

I, all about me, every breath of air, every molecule in my universe—nothing but counterfeit reality. A simulated environment designed by some vaster world of absolute existence.

★TEN★

THE AWFUL CONCEPT BATTERED THE very foundations of reason. Every person and object, the walls about me, the ground underfoot, each star out to the farthest infinity—all nothing but ingenious contrivances. An analog environment. A simulectronic creation. A world of intangible illusion. A balanced interplay of electronic charges racing off tapes and drums, leaping from cathodes to anodes, picking up the stimuli of biasing grids.

Cringing before a suddenly horrible, hostile universe, I watched without feeling as Whitney's assistants dragged his unconscious, Ashton-possessed body away. I stood by as though paralyzed while they successfully completed the re-transfer operation.

I fought my way back to the office through a fog of stupefying concepts. Fuller and I had built an analog creation so nearly perfect that our subjective reaction units would never know theirs wasn't a valid, material universe. And all the while *our* entire universe was merely the simulectronic product of a Higher World!

That was the basic discovery Fuller had stumbled upon. As a result, he had been eliminated. But he had left behind the Achilles-tortoise sketch and had somehow conveyed the information to Lynch.

And everything that had happened since then had been the result of the Operator's reprograming to cover up Fuller's discovery!

Now I could understand Jinx's behavior. She had learned the true nature of our reality from her father's notes, which she later destroyed. But she realized her only hope for safety lay in hiding her knowledge.

89

Along with every other ID unit, however, she had been stripped of all recollection of Morton Lynch.

Then, sometime yesterday, They had discovered she *knew*. And They had temporarily yanked her. They had deactivated her circuit during the night to administer special reorientation!

That was why she had been so casual, so untroubled on the videophone this morning! She was no longer terrified over the prospect of being permanently deprogramed.

But, I asked myself desperately, why had They skipped over *me* in the general reorientation following Lynch's disappearance?

I brushed straggling hair off my forehead and gazed out on my counterfeit world. It screamed back at me that what assailed my eyes was only a subjective, simulectronic illusion. I cast about for something that would blunt the impact of that staggering realization.

Even if it *were* a physical, material world, wouldn't it *still* be but nothing? Billions of light years out to the remotest star in the farthest galaxy extended a vast, almost completely empty sea, strewn here and there with infinitesimal specks of something called "matter." But even matter itself was as intangible as the endless void between the far-flung stars and planets and island universes. It was composed, in the final analysis, of "subatomic" particles, which were actually only immaterial "charges." Was that concept so untenably alien to the one discovered by Dr. Fuller—that matter and motion were but reflections of electronic charges in a simulator?

I spun around as the door from the staff section opened.

Collingsworth stood staring at me. "I watched you earlier this afternoon when they were rescuing Chuck from Simulacron-3."

Earlier this afternoon? I looked outside. It *was* getting dark. I had spent hours wrestling with my foundering thoughts.

He crossed the room and drew up solicitously before me. "Doug, you've been having more trouble, haven't you?"

Unconsciously, I nodded. Perhaps I was reaching out for whatever slim reassurance he might offer, as he had done once before. But then I caught myself. God, I couldn't tell him! If I did, he might be the next candidate for a disappearance act or an accident.

"No!" I almost shouted. "Everything's fine! Leave me alone."

"All right, we'll do it my way." He pulled up a chair. "When we spoke in my study that night I took off on the assumption you were suffering from a guilt complex—compunction over manipulating re-actional units who imagine they are real. Since then I've done some thinking on how that complex might further express itself."

The light played upon his thick, white hair, giving him a benign appearance. "I deduced what sort of obsession would result—has prob-ably already resulted—from those circumstances."

"Yes?" I looked up, only remotely interested.

"The next development would be for you to start believing that, just as *you* are manipulating *your* ID units, there is a *greater simulectronicist* in a greater world manipulating *you—all of us.*"

I leaped up. "You know! How did you find out?"

But he only smiled complacently. "The point, Doug, is—how did *you* find out?"

Even though I realized the knowledge would endanger Avery too, I told him exactly what Ashton had said on bursting into my office in the person of Chuck Whitney. I had to tell someone.

When I had finished, he squinted. "Most ingenious. I couldn't have conceived of a better device for self-deception."

"You mean Ashton didn't say this world is an illusion?"

"Do you have any witness to prove he *did*?" He paused. "Isn't it odd that the one common denominator in all your experiences is that none of them can be substantiated?"

Why was he trying to knock down every structure of reason I had erected? Had he, too, had access to Fuller's "basic discovery"? Was he steering me back to safety in ignorance?

More important, if both he and Jinx had somehow come into pos-session of the fatal information, why had she been purged of it while he had been allowed to remain unreprogramed?

Then I saw through the woods: Collingsworth was merely *aware* of my suspicions about the true nature of our world. He did not *believe* them. And therein lay his apparent immunity to being yanked.

Still, *I* hadn't rejected that lethal knowledge. Yet here I sat—unyanked, unreoriented, unreprogramed. Why?

Collingsworth placed one splayed set of fingers thoughtfully against the other. "Your rationalization processes are slow, Doug. Right now I'm even going to add another building block to your structure of pseudoparanoid obsession."

I glanced up. "What's that?"

"You overlooked rationalizing your blackouts into the pattern."

I thought of the several times I had fought off sudden seizures of near unconsciousness. "What about them?"

He shrugged. "If I were trying to weave your web of fantasy, I would say that the blackouts were the side effects of an upper world simulectronic operator establishing empathic coupling with me. A faulty coupling. You've seen it happen in your own simulator. The ID unit becomes aware *something* is going on."

I gaped. "That's it, Avery! That's exactly it! That's the one thing that explains why I haven't been yanked yet!"

He grinned, a superior there-didn't-I-tell-you-so expression. Patiently, he said, "Yes, Doug? Go on."

"It makes everything simple! The last time I had a near blackout was just last night. Do you know what I was thinking then? I was utterly convinced that everything that had happened to me had been a hallucination, just as you suggested!"

Collingsworth nodded, but not without conveying his sarcasm. "The Great Simulectronicist realized then that He didn't have to worry about reprograming you any longer?"

"Exactly! I had reprogramed myself with my own skepticism."

"And what's the next reasonable deduction in that chain of spurious logic, Doug?"

I thought a moment, then said grimly, "That I'll be safe until He decides to make another spot check and see whether I've gone back to my former convictions!"

He slapped his thigh triumphantly. "There. And you should suspect by now that that's just the still-rational part of Douglas Hall admitting he'd better get a grip on himself before those obsessions become uncontrollable."

"I know what I saw!" I protested. "I know what I heard!"

He didn't try to hide his pity. "Have it your own way. This is something I can't do for you."

I walked to the window and stared out into the night sky, ablaze with summer's canopy of familiar stars arrayed in their eons-old constellations.

Even now I was glancing hundreds of light years into space, billions upon billions of miles. Yet suppose I could pace off the absolute dimensions of my universe, as it actually existed within the bounds of the simulectronic apparatus that supported it. Would I find that all creation was compressed into an Upper Reality building that was only, say, two hundred feet long by a hundred feet in depth, as measured by the yardstick of that Higher World?

There—Ursa Major. If I could see through the illusion, would I be staring instead at nothing more than a function generator? And over there—Cassiopeia? Or actually a bulky data processor, standing next to its allocator, Andromeda?

Collingsworth's hand descended gently on my shoulder. "You can still fight it, Doug. All you have to do is make yourself see how impossible your obsessions are."

He was right, of course. I had simply to convince myself that I had only imagined Phil Ashton's mocking recital, his scornful insistence that my own world was but a simulectronic counterfeit.

"I can't do it, Avery," I said finally. "It all fits together too neatly. Ashton *did* tell me that. And it *was* the information Fuller had hidden deep in his own simulator."

"Very well, son." His shoulders fell. "If I can't stop you, then I'm going to help you put yourself through the complete works as quickly as possible."

When I only stared back nonplussed, he continued, "It's not difficult to reason what you're going to do now. But, since it'll take you three or four days to conceive of that next step, I'm going to save you the time. Eventually you'll push the analogy another notch. If this is a simulectronic creation, you'll tell yourself, then there must be someone with total knowledge of the setup working on the inside."

"The same way we have Ashton serving as a Contact Unit!"

"Right. And you'll realize sooner or later that flushing out *this* world's Phil Ashton will be the final measure of the validity of your suspicions."

I immediately saw what he was suggesting. The Upper Reality would have to have a special ID unit down here to keep an eye on developments that might not otherwise come to Their attention until some output collator was periodically checked. If I could find the Contact Unit, I might get a final, positive admission from him.

But then what? Was I to leave him to his devices afterward? Let him go free to report, on his next contact with the Upper World Operator, what I knew? I saw instantly that tracking him down was only half the job. The moment I identified him, I would have to kill him in order to protect myself.

"So," Collingsworth said soberly, "go on off in search of your Contact Unit. And good hunting, son."

"But it could be *anybody!*"

"Of course. However, if there is such a person, he would have to be close to you, wouldn't he? Why? Because all the effects you claim to have experienced apply exclusively to you."

It could be one of *many* persons. Siskin? Dorothy Ford? She had been right there when Lynch had vanished! And she had moved in to post close watch over me just as matters had become critical! Chuck Whitney? Why not? Hadn't he admittedly been the only one around when the thermite charge had gone off in the modulator? Or Marcus Heath, who was to supplant me in REIN? Or even Wayne Hartson? They had both shown up at a convenient time, during a period when the Upper Reality would have found it necessary to keep me under closer surveillance.

Jinx? Of course not. It was clear she had gone through the same routine They were putting me through.

But what about *Avery Collingsworth?* As I glanced suspiciously at him, he must have surmised my thoughts.

"Yes, Doug," he said. "Even me. By all means, you must include me, if your research is going to be thorough."

Was he sincere? Had he actually foreseen my paranoid reactions? Or was he merely being cunning for some undecipherable purpose? Was he steering me into a certain channel of action?

"Even you," I repeated profoundly.

He turned to leave but paused in the doorway. "Of course, it'll occur to you that your search will have to be made under a guise of total normalcy. You can't go about accusing people of being a Contact Unit. Because if you *are* right, it won't be long before you *will* be yanked. Correct?"

I only stared back as he closed the door behind him. But he was right. I could expect immunity at least until the next time the Operator decided to run another empathy-coupling check on me—but only if I didn't attract His attention *before* then.

◼

Outside, I was oblivious to the slight chill of night as I made my way past the late-shift reaction monitor pickets and headed for the parking lot. There was little within me that was either calm or rational. These buildings, the stars above. Just the flick of a switch would cancel them all out in an abrupt neutralization of electrical charges. And myself along with everything else.

As I continued on toward the nearest company car I thought contemptuously of all the petty human values and intricacies, ambitions, hopes, devices. Of Siskin reaching for the world and not knowing it was as tenuous as the air around him. Of the Association of Reaction Monitors, fighting Siskin's simulator to the death, not even aware that they enjoyed no greater degree of physical being than the reactional units in that machine.

But I thought mainly of the Master Simulectronicist, that metempirical Omnipotent Being who sat arrogant and secure in the immense data-processing department of His Super Simulator, allocating and integrating stimuli and putting His analog creatures through their paces.

Deus ex machina.

All was asham. All was utterly hopeless and inconsequential against the backdrop of unsuspected illusion.

"Doug!"

I drew back cautiously, squinting at the air car from which the voice had come.

"Doug, it's Jinx."

Then I remembered she had insisted upon meeting me here. Uncertainly, I went over. She reached across the seat and opened the door and the interior lights flashed on.

"You really look as if you've had it," she said, laughing.

Which reminded me it had been two days since I'd had any sleep. And I could feel a numbing fatigue undermining even the horrifying comprehensions of that impossible day.

"Rough afternoon," I said, climbing in beside her.

I glanced into her face and was instantly impressed with the change that had come over her. During the past few days I had only *imagined* she was attractive. I saw now that she was. For all that while her elegant features had been laden with the effects of terrifying knowledge. Now it was clear that she had been relieved of that burden. In place of her troubled expression was a winsome cast of loveliness.

"In that case," she said with a spritelike smile that was reminiscent of the fifteen-year-old Jinx's effervescence, "we'll cancel plan number one and settle for the alternative."

The car rose skyward in a swift, swaying motion that almost put me to sleep as the brilliance of the city fanned out all around us.

"We were going to go back to that little restaurant," she explained. "But not now. You need a quiet evening at home."

I had to act perfectly natural, Collingsworth had suggested. If, by chance, They brought me under surveillance I would have to convince Them I was still an unsuspecting part of the illusion. Even now that Real World Operator could be studying me through Jinx's eyes, listening to me through her ears.

"Sounds fine," I agreed, with perhaps exaggerated enthusiasm. "In its domestic simplicity, the evening could be a taste of things to come."

"Why, Mr. Hall!" she said coyly. "That sounds like a left-handed proposal."

I moved closer, took her hand and caressed it. If that Operator were looking in now, I was determined, suspicion over my actions would be the last thing that would occur to Him.

She put together a light supper—nothing elaborate, nothing conventional—and we ate in the kitchen as though we were old hands at domestic informality.

Only once during the meal did I drift off into abstraction. That was to peck away stubbornly at the one remaining inconsistency: Why hadn't They reoriented me at the moment They saw I might come into possession of Fuller's "basic discovery"? They had meticulously reprogramed Jinx, deleting from her retentive circuits all data that had any bearing on the forbidden knowledge. But They hadn't stopped her from coming into contact with the one ID unit who might lead her back to awareness of the fatal information—me.

"Doug, you *are* exhausted, aren't you?"

I sat up alertly. "I suppose I am."

She took my hand and led me into the study, over to the inviting leather couch. I lay with my head in her lap and she stroked my temple with a delicate, tender motion.

"I could sing something gentle," she proposed, joking.

"You do," I said for the benefit of Whoever might be watching and listening, "whenever you talk."

Then, unwittingly, I rang the curtain down on my special perfor-mance as I stared up into her vivid, intense eyes. I brought her head down and kissed her and, for a moment that was an eternity in itself, I forgot all about simulectronic mockeries, an Upper Reality, an Om-nipotent Operator, a world of nothingness. Here was something tan-gible, a mooring buoy in a lashing sea.

Eventually sleep came. But only under a pall of fear that the Opera-tor would decide to run another spot check on my convictions before I could flush out His Contact Unit.

✳ELEVEN✳

HALFWAY TO REACTIONS THE NEXT morning I punched in a new destination on the air car's control panel. The craft nosed around, then headed for the great, towering hulk of Babel Central, which rose haughtily above the layer of puffball clouds that it wore like a peplum.

I felt a sort of trivial pride over the fact that I had not yet run amuck, as had Cau No in his own counterfeit world. Even as I had awakened in Jinx's study, I had wondered whether I might manage to bury Fuller's discovery deep in my mind—so deep that it wouldn't be detectable during an empathic coupling.

But *could* I settle back into a normal pattern, knowing what I knew? Could I bury my head in the sand and merely accept whatever fate the Higher Powers programed into Their simulator for me? Of course not. I had to find the Contact Unit in this world, if there was one. And Siskin was as good a starting point as any.

The car fell into a hovering pattern while waiting for two other vehicles to cushion off from Babel Central's landing shelf.

Absently, my gaze went out to the haze-shrouded countryside east of the city. And I recalled the night I had ridden with Jinx to the fringe of a terrifying, infinite nothingness—and witnessed the creation of half a universe. I realized now that here was another inconsistency which defied explanation. Unless—

Of course! A simulectronic world depends upon the Gestalt principle for its verisimilitude—the presence of a sufficient number of items in a pattern to suggest the entire pattern. The cognitive whole is greater than the sum of its perceptible parts. The missing landscape had simply been one of the "gaps" in reality. Gaps that wouldn't *normally* be encountered by reactional units.

Even in Fuller's simulator, the possibility existed that an ID unit might come upon an unfinished bit of "scenery." Such a discovery, however, triggered automatic reprograming circuits that not only immediately "created" the needed item, but also stripped from the reactional entity the memory of having encountered a missing prop.

For my benefit, the road and countryside had been "filled in" on the spot. But why hadn't I been reoriented to believe there had been nothing wrong in the first place?

The car landed and I made my way along a hedge-lined flagstone lane that led directly to Siskin's office. There his receptionist scanned me with the superior stare that personnel of the Inner Establishment reserved for those of the Outer and announced me.

Siskin himself strode out and took me by the arm to lead me back inside. He was exuberant as he perched on the desk, legs dangling.

"I was just going to call you," he said. "You may not have to dress up the Siskin image too much, after all, when you program it into our machine. I've been accepted as a member of the party's Central Committee!"

He seemed only slightly disappointed that I didn't gape over the development. But that didn't discourage him.

"And what's more, Doug, there's already speculation on my having a shot at the governor's seat!"

Thoughtfully, he added, "But, of course, I won't be satisfied with anything like that. Sixty-four, you know. Can't live forever. Got to move fast."

In a moment of precipitous decision, I stepped squarely in front of him. "All right, Siskin. You can put aside the mask. *I know!*"

Starting, he drew back from the severity in my stare. He glanced frantically at the intercom, the ceiling, back into my eyes.

"You *know?*" His voice quaked as I had expected the Contact Unit's would when I finally confronted him.

"You didn't think I wouldn't eventually figure it out?"

"How did you find out? Did Heath tell you? Dorothy?"

"They both know too?"

"Well, they had to, didn't they?"

My fingers worked restlessly. I had to verify the identification. Then I had to kill him before he could report to the Simulectronicist in that Upper Reality that I had slipped my puppet strings.

"You mean," I asked, "that there are *three* Contact Units?"

He raised an eyebrow. "What in hell are we talking about?"

I wasn't so sure now. "Suppose you tell me."

"Doug, I had to do it—for my own protection. You realize that, of course. When Dorothy told me you intended to betray me and the party, I had to take countermeasures."

All the tenseness drained out of me. We hadn't been talking about the same thing after all.

"Sure, I brought in Heath," he continued, "in case you became intractable and had to be dumped. You can't blame me for protecting my own interest."

"No," I managed.

"I wasn't lying when I said I like you. It's just unfortunate you can't see everything my way. But it's not too late. As I said, Heath is merely my ace in the hole. I don't *want* to use him."

Disinterested, I headed for the door, aware that locating the Contact Unit might not be as simple as I had imagined.

"What are you going to do, son?" he asked softly, following after me. "Don't try anything stupid. I've got a lot of strings handy. But I wouldn't relish pulling them—not against you."

I turned and faced him. It was more than evident now that he wasn't the Contact Unit. The ambiguity in our conversation, at the outset, had struck close enough to home to have flushed him out if he had been. Moreover, a Contact Unit would know infinite frustration. He would be endlessly appalled over the futility of all things. He would be withdrawn, philosophical. Siskin? Never. He was too motivated by the material—wealth, possessiveness, ambition.

"I haven't given up on you, Doug. You can reinstate yourself. Just say the word and I'll drop Heath. I'll even call off Dorothy. All you have to do is prove you've changed your mind about me."

"How?" I asked superficially.

"Go before my own notarypsych with me for a complete affirmation probe."

More as a means of getting away than for any other reason, I said,

"I'll think about it."

On the way back to REIN, I gave only passing attention to what had happened in Siskin's office. It was obvious he was merely executing a delaying movement. He was holding out the promise of forgiveness and acceptance only as a means of discouraging me from making a public issue of his political schemes.

But if I posed such a threat, why didn't he simply pull his police strings and have me arrested for Fuller's murder? True, that would deprive the simulator of many refinements Fuller and I had planned together. But certainly he must have guessed by now that the system was equal to the task of mapping foolproof political strategy even without further improvement.

Then, as the car began its descent along the vertical control beam nearest Reactions, Inc., I tensed under the impact of fresh, disconcerting suspicion. Was *Siskin* manipulating the police—to prevent me from betraying him? Or were the police actually an unwitting agency *of the Higher Existence*, poised to arrest me for Fuller's murder the moment the Operator became aware I had learned the true nature of reality?

I sank miserably back against the seat. I was hopelessly confused, squeezed between the calculating malevolence of two worlds, so utterly confounded that I couldn't recognize whether any particular assault was coming from one or the other.

And all the while I had to maintain my composure. For the simplest demonstration of the fact that I knew about the existence of the Real World might result in my being immediately yanked into the oblivion of total deprograming.

At Reactions, I found Marcus Heath seated at my desk, poring over two stacks of memoranda he had rifled from the drawers.

I studded the door closed and he looked up through his bifocals. There was no uneasiness in his intense eyes. It was clear he didn't consider that he had been caught red-handed.

"Yes?" he said impatiently.

"What are you doing here?"

"This is my office now. Orders straight from the Inner Establishment. For the time being you'll find desk space with Mr. Whitney in the function generating department."

Understandably indifferent to so prosaic a development, I turned to leave. At the door, however, I hesitated. Now was as good a time as any for finding out whether *he* was the Contact Unit.

"What do you want?" he asked irritably.

I returned to the desk and scanned his frozen features, wondering whether I was finally about to prove I didn't exist. Then I rebelled against the utter incongruity of that thought. I *had* to exist! Cartesian philosophy provided ample refutation of my self-doubt:

Cogito ergo sum: I think, therefore I am.

"Don't waste my time," Heath said, annoyed. "I've got to get this simulator ready for public demonstration within a week."

Sweeping irresolution aside, I straightened. "You can quit acting. I know you're an agent for that other simulator."

He only remained rigid. But there had been an inner upheaval. I could tell by the sudden ferocity in his eyes. Then I realized that at this very moment he might be coupled empathically with his Operator in that Upper Reality!

Calmly, he asked, "What did you say?"

Now he wanted me to repeat it for the benefit of the Operator! Already my delay had been fatal!

I lunged across the desk, reaching out desperately for him. But he lurched back out of range and his hand came up from the drawer with a laser gun.

The broad crimson beam fanned out at my arms, my chest, my abdomen and I slumped across the desk, instantly deprived of all muscular control from waist to neck.

It was simple for him to haul me upright and set me upon my feet. Then he forced me backwards toward a chair and shoved me into it. With the laser gun he sprayed my legs.

I sat there slumped sideways, able to move only my head. Frantically, I tried to work my arm to determine how complete the paralysis was. Only my index finger twitched. That meant I'd be immobile for hours. And all he needed was minutes. I could but sit there and await deprograming.

"When will it happen?" I asked hopelessly.

He didn't answer. After a moment he studded home the locks on both doors. Then he leaned against the edge of the desk.

"How did you find it out, Hall?"

I hadn't spent a conscious minute over the past day without

102

wondering how I would react on finding myself trapped in just such a final confrontation. Now that it was here, I wasn't nearly as terrified as I had imagined I would be.

"From Fuller," I said.

"But how could he have known?"

"He's the one who found out. You must know that much."

"Why should I?"

"Then there's more than one agent?"

"If there is, they've kept it a damned good secret from me."

He glanced at the intercom, then back at me. It was evident he was troubled over something. But I couldn't imagine what. He had surely discharged his function creditably, as far as the Higher Reality was concerned.

Then he smiled as he returned and seized a handful of my hair. He forced my head back and sprayed my throat lightly.

Again I was perplexed. If I was going to be yanked at any moment, why was he temporarily paralyzing my vocal cords?

He ran a comb through his hair and straightened his coat. Settling back in his chair, he spoke softly into the intercom:

"Miss Ford, will you please get Mr. Siskin on video? And put the call on a security circuit."

I couldn't see the screen. But Siskin's voice was unmistakable as he asked, "Any trouble over there, Marcus?"

"No. Everything's in hand. Horace, you've given me a damned nice setup here and things are going to be profitable for both of us because we see eye to eye—on all matters." Heath hesitated.

"Yes?"

"That's important, Horace—the fact that we *do* see eye to eye. About the party and everything else. I'm stressing that point because tomorrow I want to appear with you before a notarypsych."

I was becoming more confused. Not only had I not been deprogramed, but this conversation was completely irrelevant.

"Now hold on," Siskin protested. "I don't see why I should have to validate anything I said to you."

"You don't." Heath's features were heavy with sincerity and subservience. "It's I who must convince you that henceforth I'll be the most loyal cog in your organization. It's not only that I appreciate a good deal when it's dumped in my lap. The main reason is that you and I belong together—on the same side."

"You're not making much sense, Marcus. What's on your mind?"

"Simply this: I came over here as an agent for that other simulator project."

"Barnfeld?"

Heath nodded. "I've been in their pay right along. I was supposed to steal all of Reaction's secrets, so Barnfeld could perfect a simulator that would rival yours."

Even in the grip of laserparalysis, I finally understood. Once more I had leaped recklessly at an ambiguity. Heath had been an inside simulectronic agent, all right, but only for a rival simulator in *this* world.

"And did you?" Siskin asked, interested.

"No, Horace. And I never intended to. Not since the second discussion I had with you about coming here. The notarypsych will verify that."

Siskin remained silent.

"Don't you see, Horace? I *want* to be loyal to you. Almost from the beginning I've wanted to serve you in whatever capacity I can. It was only a matter of deciding when to make a clean breast and ask for a notarypsych probe."

"And what decided you?"

"When Hall burst in here a few minutes ago to say he knew about my connections with Barnfeld and to threaten to expose me."

There was amusement hanging on Siskin's words as he said, "And you're ready to verify all this before a psych?"

"Any time. Right now if you want."

"Tomorrow will be soon enough." Then Siskin laughed delightedly. "Barnfeld planting an agent here! Can you imagine that? Very well, Marcus. You'll stay on—if the notary gives us an affirmative, of course. And you'll supply Barnfeld with all the supposedly secret information he wants. Only, we'll see that it's the type of false data that will bust him completely."

Heath disconnected and came over. "Now, Hall, you don't have your hatchet any longer, do you? Even worse, you're going to feel like hell after that laser spraying." He paused and savored his triumph. "I'll have Gadsen send you home."

Neither Siskin nor Heath had been the Contact Unit. Whom

would I try next? Frankly, I didn't know. The Unit, I saw at last, could be *anyone*—even the most insignificant file clerk. And I was hopelessly convinced that long before my search was over I would find myself suddenly reeling under the head-splitting impact of the inevitable next empathy coupling. The Operator would then find out that I knew all about His Upper Reality.

✹ TWELVE ✹

STREAMS OF LIQUID FIRE RACED one another through my veins all during the night as the after-effects of the laser spraying ran their excruciating course. I might have hidden the pain beneath a tide of vindictive rancor for Heath. But I had long since lost the delusion that petty physical matters might still be of importance.

Shortly before midmorning, the guard whom Gadsen had detailed to my apartment helped me out of bed and led me into the kitchen. He had punched out a light breakfast from the autoserver. Nothing substantial. My stomach wouldn't have been able to handle it.

After he left, I munched on a corner of equitoast and swallowed some coffee. Then I sat there wondering whether it would ever be possible to adjust to the knowledge Fuller had bequeathed me.

I was nothing—merely a package of vital simulectronic charges. Nevertheless I *had* to exist. Simple logic demanded no less. I think, therefore I am. But then I wasn't the *first* person to be troubled by the possibility that nothing is real. How about the solipsists, the Berkeleians, the transcendentalists? Throughout the ages, objective reality had been held up to the closest scrutiny. Subjectivists were far from the exception in efforts to understand the true nature of existence. And even pure science had swung heavily to phenomenalism, with its principle of indeterminacy, its concept that the observed is inseparable from the observer.

Indeed, ontology was never lacking in its tribute to conceptualism. Plato saw ultimate reality existing only as pure ideas. For Aristotle, matter was a passive nonsubstance upon which thought acted to produce reality. In essence, the latter definition wasn't too far removed from the concept of an ID unit's subjective capacity, biasing and being biased by its simulectronic environment.

My newly acquired appreciation of fundamental reality required only one ultimate concession: Doomsday, when it came, wouldn't be a physical phenomenon; it would be an all-inclusive erasure of simulectronic circuits.

And of all the metaphysical concepts that had cropped up during the long course of philosophy, mine was the only one open to final verification. It could be proved conclusively by merely finding the teleological agent—the hidden Contact Unit.

By noon, a hot shower and airblast rubdown had taken out the final kinks and I had returned to Reactions.

In the central corridor Chuck Whitney stepped from the function generating department and caught my arm. "Doug! What's going on?" he asked. "Why is Heath installed in your office?"

"Let's just say I locked horns with Siskin."

"Well, if you don't want to discuss it …." He stepped into function generation and beckoned for me to follow. "I'm supposed to show you where you'll hang your hat from now on."

He led me past the huge master data integrator and down a row of bulky input allocators, each squat cabinet standing like a somber sentry with hundreds of blinking eyes and whirling discs.

We reached the other end of the room and he indicated a glass-walled cubbyhole. "Make yourself at home."

We went in and I spent a moment surveying my newly decreed austerity. Bare oak floor, unpolished. One desk with a fold-away vocascriber to handle my own correspondence. Two straight-back chairs. One filing cabinet.

Chuck straddled the extra chair. "Siskin was here this morning. Brought in two new assistants for Heath. As I understand it, he's set on a public demonstration of the simulator as soon as possible."

"Probably wants to nail down public sentiment with a big show."

He said, "You're on the way out, Doug. Why?"

I sank into the other chair. "Siskin has his own ideas about how the simulator should be used. I don't agree with them."

"If there's anything I can do, just sound off."

Whitney—the Contact Unit? Someone I'd known for years? My best friend? Well, why not? In our own simulator Phil Ashton had close acquaintances too. None of *them* suspected *his* true nature.

"Chuck," I asked pensively, "how would you contrast the perceptual processes involved when we see, say, a chair, with those that take place when an ID unit sees the simulectronic equivalent of a chair?"

"This going to be a brain-twisting session?" He laughed.

"Seriously, what's the difference?"

"Well, in our case a 2-D image of the chair is projected onto the retina. It's scanned neurologically and broken down into a series of sensory impulses that are sent directly to the brain. Coded information. Linear transfer."

"And with the ID unit?"

"The analog chair is actually a pattern of stored impulses. When the unit simulectronically comes into 'visual' contact with the chair, one of its perceptual circuits is biased by those impulses. That circuit in turn transmits them to the unit's memory drums."

"How efficient is the ID's perceptual system?"

"Compares favorably with ours. Each of its drums stores over seven million bits and completes a revolution in two-thousandths of a second. As a result, recognition and reaction times are roughly equivalent to ours."

I leaned back, watching his face carefully, wondering whether he suspected I was leading him down a forbidden lane. "And what happens when an ID unit goes off the deep end?"

"Goes irrational?" He hunched his shoulders. "An allocator gets out of phase. The ID's perceptual circuits receive conflicting impulses. Something that isn't supposed to be there crops up—or vanishes. Suspicious, operating under faulty modulation, he begins to notice the chinks in his simulated environment."

Suddenly emboldened, I suggested, "Such as stumbling upon a road, a sweep of countryside, and half a galaxy that aren't there?"

"Sure. Something like that."

He said it without even twitching an eyelid. As far as I was concerned, he had passed the test.

On the other hand, wouldn't a Contact Unit, conditioned by the Upper Reality Operator, be just that efficient?

Then, as I stared out through the glass partition into the function generating department, I tensed with the realization that at that very moment I was looking at one of the "environmental chinks."

Seeing my expression, Whitney cast a puzzled glance out into the room. "What is it?"

Immediately I recognized the opportunity for a second test, to establish more fully that he was not the Contact Unit. I laughed. "I just noticed something odd about our master data integrator."

He studied it momentarily. "I don't see anything."

"The cabinet is a single, welded unit. I think I can call off its dimensions. Five and a half by twelve. A little over ten feet high. You remember when we installed it?"

"Ought to. I directed the crew."

"But, Chuck, there isn't a door or window in this room large enough for something that size to pass through!"

He was confused for a second. Then he laughed and pointed. "Unless it would be that rear door opening on the parking lot."

I kept a straight face as I turned and looked. There *was* a door there—large enough to have admitted the integrator. But it hadn't been there a moment ago!

Chuck's perplexed reaction had triggered an automatic adjustment circuit. That only I was able to remember the time when the door had *not* been there was evidence of the fact that I was still, for some reason, exempt from reorientation.

The intercom sounded. I flicked it on and Dorothy Ford's tense face lighted the screen. She glanced uneasily at Chuck.

"Got some work to do," he said accommodatingly and left.

I watched Dorothy wage a pitched battle with distress. Her eyes moistened and her fingers entwined nervously. "Would it help any if I said I was sorry?" she asked.

"You told Siskin I planned to cross him up?"

She nodded ashamedly. "Yes, Doug. I had to."

And I knew, from the sincerity in her voice, that betraying me was the last thing she had wanted to do.

She went on soberly. "I warned you, didn't I? I made it clear I had to look out for Siskin's interest."

"You rate an E for efficiency."

"Yes, I suppose I do. But I'm not proud of my performance."

So she had admitted exposing me to Siskin. Would she also eventually own up to selling me out to a Power far greater?

I laughed. "We're not going to let it drop there, are we?"

She frowned in puzzlement.

"Well," I went on, "you once said we both had our jobs but that there was no reason why we couldn't have fun at the same time."

She only lowered her head, apparently in sudden disappointment.

"Oh, I see." I feigned bitterness. "The setup isn't the same. Now that you've achieved your objective, I'm no longer fair game."

"No. That's not it, Doug."

"But certainly you've discharged your obligation commendably and you don't have to keep an eye on me from now on."

"No, I don't. Siskin is well satisfied."

Pretending impatience, I started to snap off the intercom.

She leaned forward anxiously. "No, wait!"

Merely a girl who was disillusioned because the supposedly modest fellow for whom she had made a play in her line of duty had decided to take her up on it? Or a Contact Unit in fear of losing her direct line of communication with the subject under surveillance?

"All right," she said unenthusiastically. "We can have fun."

"When?"

She hesitated. "Whenever you say."

At the moment, I couldn't imagine a more likely suspect in my search for the Contact Unit. This one I would check out properly. "Tonight," I suggested. "At your place."

Dorothy Ford's apartment was one of those soft, opulent sanctums that have traditionally been associated with the libertine privileges of wealthy businessmen. Letting me come here, I saw from the beginning, was but another humiliation for the girl.

Tri-D animated murals, each with its own background music, flaunted suggestive scenery. Pan piped and kicked up his cloven hoofs while uninhibited maidens ringed him in with their sensuous dance of abandon. Aphrodite embraced Adonis between a pair of marble columns festooned with climbing roses and framing a glistening Aegean Sea in the distance. Cleopatra, dark hair radiant with the soft caress of moonlight reflecting off the Nile, raised a jeweled goblet to toast Mark

Antony, then leaned back against the railing of her barge.

Overseeing all was a huge tri-D portrait of Horace P. Siskin. I stared up at the painting, recognizing now a facet of the man's character of which I hadn't been aware. His eyes, as they bored into the Aphrodite-Adonis mural, were vivid in lecherous intent. His entire expression added up to only one inescapable impression: satyriasis.

The euphonious enchantment of the room was shattered as Dorothy punched the order button on the autotender. Receiving her drink, she swilled half of it, then stared abstractedly into her glass, as though trying to find something she had lost long ago. She wore pastel blue lounging pajamas, trimmed in ermine. Her hair, upswept and aglitter with sparkle-spray, was like a soft crown of stardust that somehow imparted a fresh, innocent appearance to her chiseled face. But there was calm determination in her features. She had committed herself to a bargain. And now she was going to carry out her end.

Strolling over, she gestured toward Siskin's portrait. "I can draw the drapes and cut him off. I often do."

"Cut him off from all these things that belong to him?"

She winced. "He's no longer interested. Once they meant something. But, then, vitality isn't a permanent thing."

"You sound regretful."

"God, no."

She went over and dialed herself another bracer, leaving me standing there perplexed. Would a Contact Unit allow herself to become involved in unconventional complications?

She drained the fresh drink, waited for another, then returned. The alcohol was beginning to have its effects. Her spirit seemed somewhat higher, although a certain trace of sullenness remained.

"Here's to the Great Little One." She raised her glass, sipped from it, then stepped back and hurled it at the portrait.

It shattered against Siskin's left cheek, leaving a gash in the canvas that continued the wry slit of his mouth. The liquid content of the glass appeared to be pouring from both.

"Now I didn't want to do that, Doug." She laughed dryly. "You'll think I'm not a good sport."

"Why did you let me come here?"

She shrugged and lied. "For the atmosphere. You won't find a more appropriate setting anywhere in the city. Siskin's taste, such as it is, can't be beat."

When she headed back for the bar I caught her arm. She turned, swayed slightly and stared piercingly into my eyes.

"I gave you a warning once before when I wasn't supposed to," she said. "Have another on the house. You don't want to have anything to do with me. I brought you up here so you'd realize that for yourself."

Despite my own compelling purpose for calling on her, I found myself being drawn involuntarily into the enigma of Dorothy Ford. And, with a sense of pity, I wondered what strange requirement of special programing was responsible for her character.

"When was Siskin here last?" I asked.

"Two years ago."

"And you're disappointed?"

Indignation flared in her eyes and she snapped my head aside with a stinging slap. She went over to the *chaise contour* and buried her face in its cushioned depths.

I followed. "I'm sorry, Dorothy."

"Don't be. I went in with my eyes open."

"No you didn't. That's obvious. What happened?"

She looked up and stared through the Antony-Cleopatra mural. "I often imagine I have no more power of self-determination than one of the characters in your machine. There are times when I *feel* like one of them. I even have horrible dreams about Siskin sitting in front of Simulacron-3 and making me perform like a puppet."

I knew then that Dorothy Ford *couldn't* be the Contact Unit. The last thing such an agent would do would be to hint, however remotely, at the true circumstances of reality. Instead, she had hit the nail almost on the head.

"No," she went on distantly. "I'm no nymphomaniac. There's been only Siskin. You see, my father is one of the corporate directors of the Establishment. And Dad will continue to be the financial genius he imagines he is only as long as I hop through Siskin's hoop."

"You mean your father's a success only because you—"

She nodded miserably. "That's the only reason. When Siskin took him in five years ago, Dad was recovering from a heart attack. He couldn't survive the knowledge of what the set-up has been."

She started as the door buzzer sounded. I went over and flicked on the one-way video screen.

The man in the corridor had a pad ready when he identified himself. "James Ross, CRM Number 2317-B3. For Miss Dorothy Ford."

It was most coincidental that just when I was trying to establish whether Dorothy was the Contact Unit a monitor should appear.

"Miss Ford is ill," I said. "She can't see anyone."

"Sorry, sir. But I'll have to stand on my RM Code rights."

Then I remembered what I had seen on entering the apartment. "If you look above the pickup lens, Mr. Ross, you'll notice a certificate that says Miss Ford holds a special Evening Exemption."

Hardly glancing up, he grimaced in disappointment. "Sorry, sir. I didn't see it."

After I turned the screen off, I stood there for a long while with my hand on the switch. An honest mistake? Or was ARM involved in some special way in the Upper Reality's designs on me?

I went over to the bar, the faint beginnings of logical realization trying to break through my confusion. Besides being programed by the Higher World Operator, the Association of Reaction Monitors was in excellent position to keep close watch over not only me, but everybody else, if it wanted to.

Hadn't it been an anonymous pollster who had warned me, "For God's sake, Hall … forget about the whole damned thing"?

I dialed a drink, but left it sitting there in the delivery slot, wondering whether the monitors themselves might not be discharging some specific, unsuspected function in this counterfeit world.

Then the answer burst in upon me: Of course! Why hadn't I thought of it sooner? A simulectronic creation wouldn't exist as an end in itself. It would have to have a *raison d'être*, a primary function. The analog community Fuller and I had created was originally intended to forecast individual response as a means of assessing the marketability of commercial products.

Similarly, but on a higher plane, our entire world, the simulectronic creation in which I existed as an ID reactional unit, was but a question-and-answer device for the edification of producers, manufacturers, marketers, retailers in that Higher Reality!

The reaction monitors comprised the system whereby the Upper Operator asked His questions, introduced His stimuli! The method was analogous to Fuller's own, cruder expedient of using analog billboards, public

113

address networks, open telecasts to stimulate responses in *our* simulator!

And wasn't it only logical that the Operator would have a cognizant agent associated *directly with ARM*, the most important institution in His whole simulectronic creation?

Early next morning I cushioned down on a public parking lot two blocks away from the Association of Reaction Monitors building. Pedistripping the rest of the way, I attached to my sleeve the one object that would insure unquestioned access to ARM headquarters—the armband I had wrested from the pollster who had tried to warn me off.

At the entrance, though, there was no guard to check on the identities of the monitors flowing in for their assignments. But before I became suspicious, I reminded myself that ARM wasn't a secret organization, nor did it ostensibly have anything to hide.

In the central lobby, I paused before the directory and searched out the entry "Office of the President—3407."

I had a simple plan. I would merely ask the secretary of each official, from the top on down, to announce that a new monitor from *Upper Reality, Inc.*, was checking in with the association. If there was a Contact Unit here, the mere mention of the name of the firm I purportedly represented would flush him out.

On the thirty-fourth floor, I stepped from the elevator and ducked immediately behind a luxuriant potted plant.

Two men were just emerging from the office of the president.

But even as I tried to hide I realized that one of them had seen and recognized me.

And that one was the Contact Unit himself!

It had to be. For it was Avery Collingsworth.

✶THIRTEEN✶

COLLINGSWORTH DREW UP BESIDE THE potted plant and our eyes met, his inexpressive, steady, mine casting frantically about for an avenue of escape. But there was none.

The other man had darted back into the president's office.

"I've been expecting you," Collingsworth said evenly.

Instinct screamed out for me to kill him, quickly, before he could signal to the Operator. But I only backed against the wall.

"I knew you would eventually suppose that the Association of Reaction Monitors was the Operator's factotum in this world," the psychological consultant said. "Whenever you did, you were bound to come here looking for your Contact Unit. Right, Doug?"

Speechless, I nodded.

He smiled faintly. The expression, along with his slightly mussed, white hair and stout face, gave him an anomalous cherubic appearance.

"So you come here and find me," he went on. "I was afraid that would happen. But I don't suppose it makes any difference now. Because, you see, it's too late."

"Aren't you going to report me?" I asked, just a bit hopeful.

"Aren't *I* going to report *you*?" He laughed. "Doug, your mind won't get out of its rut, will it? You don't yet see that—"

The man who had been with him made his second emergence from the president's office. This time he had four rugged-looking reaction monitors with him.

But Collingsworth stepped in front of them. "That won't be

115

necessary," he said.

"But you said he was with Reactions!"

"Possibly he still is. But he won't be, not for long. Siskin's got him on the skids."

The man eyed me speculatively. "This is Hall?"

Collingsworth nodded. "Douglas Hall, former technical director for REIN. Doug, Vernon Carr. As you know, Carr is president of ARM."

The man extended a hand. But I drew back. Only dimly had I heard the conversation. Instead I had braced myself for the final moment when I would be summarily yanked. Would it come without warning? Or would the Operator first couple himself with me to verify my incorrigibility?

"You'll have to excuse Hall; he's not himself," Avery apologized ambiguously. "He had his own trouble to begin with. And Siskin hasn't been making things any easier."

"What are we going to do with him?" Carr asked.

Collingsworth took me by the arm and drew me across the hall toward a closed door. "Before we decide that, I'd like to speak with him alone."

He studded the door open and brought me into what was obviously a board room, with its long mahogany table bracketed by two lines of empty chairs.

Then I understood. He had to get me alone so there would be no witnesses to my deprograming!

I whirled and hit the door stud. But it was locked.

"Take it easy," Collingsworth said soothingly. "I'm no Contact Unit."

I turned incredulously to face him. "You're *not*?"

"If I were, I would have decided to have you yanked long ago, on the basis of your obstinate convictions."

"Then what *are* you doing here?"

"Forget about your damned obsession. Look at this development rationally. Isn't it understandable that my sympathies might be fully *against* Horace Siskin and his grubby enterprise? In short, I'm an agent, all right. But not in the sense you imagine. I'm aligned with ARM because I realize it's the only organization strong enough to fight Siskin's simulator."

116

Relieved but confounded at the same time, I groped my way into a chair.

Collingsworth came and stood over me. "I've been working with the reaction monitors, keeping them filled in on every move Siskin's made. That's why ARM was ready with its picketing gambit within hours after Siskin broke the news of Simulacron-3 at the party."

I glanced up. "You planted the thermite bomb?"

"Yes. But believe me, son, I didn't know you were going to be in the peephole room when it went off."

Unbelievingly, I repeated, "You've been spying against Siskin?"

Nodding, Avery said, "He's vicious, Doug. I realized what his ultimate goal was when I saw him with Hartson. But I was working with Vernon Carr long before then. I had enough sense to know you can't, with the flick of a simulectronic switch, throw millions of men out of jobs all over the country."

Convinced finally that he wasn't, after all, the Contact Unit, I lost interest in his petty intricacies. But he misinterpreted my silence for skepticism.

"We *can* fight him, son! We've got allies we don't even know about! For instance: Siskin and the party get their flunkies to introduce legislation outlawing public opinion sampling. And what happens? A bill that should have become law gets dumped for this session!"

I lunged from the chair. "Avery! Don't you realize what that *actually* means? Don't you *see* who your ally is in Congress?"

He straightened, perplexed.

"The Operator up there!" I pointed. "I should have realized it long ago. Don't you understand? The Upper Reality is not just trying to reorient or deprogram anyone who learns what the setup is. That's only one of Their purposes. *Their main target is Siskin's simulator itself! They want it destroyed!*"

"Oh, for God's sake, son!" He scowled. "Sit down and—"

"No, wait! That's it, Avery! You didn't plant the thermite bomb in the interest of ARM. You did it because you were so programed by the Operator!"

Impatiently, he asked, "Then why wasn't I programed to plant another and another, until I succeeded?"

"Because everything that's done down here has to be manipulated within a framework of reasonable cause and effect. After Siskin redoubled his security effort at REIN, it wasn't *likely* that a subversive attempt would succeed!"

"Doug," he interrupted wearily, "listen—"

"No, *you* listen! The Upper Reality doesn't want us to put our simulator into operation. Why? Because that would wipe out ARM and all its reaction monitors. And They can't have that because the pollsters are Their system for introducing reaction-seeking stimuli into this world!"

"Really, Doug, I—"

I paced in front of him. "So They go all out to eliminate Fuller's simulator. They program you to wield the hatchet. You fail. They program all of ARM. Picketing, unrest, violence will get the job done, They figure. But Siskin counters what he thinks is ARM strategy by marshaling public opinion against the pickets. And now it's stalemate. That's why the pressure's been off me lately. The Operator hasn't had time to check and see whether I'm still willing to believe I was only suffering pseudoparanoia."

"You're just rationalizing your hallucinations."

"The hell I am! I understand clearly now. And I can see I'm not the *only* one in danger!"

He smiled. "Who else? Me? Because you've—ah, contaminated me with forbidden concepts?"

"No. Not just you. *The whole world!*"

"Oh, come now." But deep furrows were beginning to show his doubt.

"Look. The Operator has tried every reasonable way of eliminating Simulacron-3—subversion, direct attack by ARM, legislation. But all His efforts have failed. He can't reprogram Siskin because then the party would take up where Siskin leaves off. He can't reprogram the party because thousands of reactional entities would be involved, right on down to the grassroots level.

"And he hasn't made a move for several days now. Which means only one thing: He's planning a final, all-out attack of some sort or other on the simulator! If it succeeds, our world will be safe again. But if it fails—"

Collingsworth leaned forward tensely in his chair. "Yes?"

Grimly, I went on. "If it fails, there's only one recourse: He'll have to destroy the entire complex! Wipe every reactional circuit clean! Deactivate His simulator—*our world*—and start over from scratch!"

Collingsworth clasped his hands together. And, terrified, I realized abruptly that I might be *convincing* him of my case! The disastrous consequences were instantly apparent:

The Operator's attention was off me at the moment. But it wasn't off Avery! Collingsworth had been insidiously programed to sabotage the simulator; to help the pollsters attack Reactions, Inc.; *even to tread along the brink of acknowledging the true nature of reality in order to convince me I was only a victim of pseudoparanoia!*

If the Operator should learn that instead *I* had convinced *Collingsworth*, then He would realize the hopelessness of trying to pull me back in line. It would mean total deprograming, oblivion, *for both Avery and me!*

Collingsworth raised his head and his eyes locked with mine.

"One of the tests of a system of logic," he said softly, "is whether the predictions it accommodates are valid. That's why I was so sure I had accurately diagnosed your symptoms. Just a moment ago, however, you made a forecast of your own. You surmised that the Operator was contriving a final, all-out attack on—"

The door opened abruptly to the accompaniment of whirring tumblers activated by a biocapacitance circuit. Vernon Carr barged in. "Damn it, Avery! Do you realize what time it is?"

"Yes," Collingsworth said distantly.

"Avery," I pleaded desperately, "forget what I just said!" I laughed. "Don't you see I was only trying to build up a case and—and show you that—"

It was no use. I had convinced him. And now the next empathy coupling between the Operator and either him or me would be fatal for both of us.

"Well, what are we going to do with Hall?" Carr asked.

Collingsworth shrugged and rose listlessly. "It really doesn't make any difference—not now."

Puzzlement seized Carr's hawklike features, but only for a moment. Then he smiled and said, "But, of course, you're right. This is it, Avery! We'll either succeed and destroy the simulator in the next half hour, or we'll fail. What Hall does between now and then *won't*

119

make any difference."

He crossed eagerly to the wall and drew back a pair of drapes, exposing a huge video screen. Somehow I sensed I was about to learn why Collingsworth had been stunned by my spontaneous prediction. Carr turned on the switch and the room was immediately engulfed in a pandemonium of tumultuous sound as whirling patches of light and shadow chased one another frantically across the face of the tube.

From a lofty vantage point, the camera zoomed down upon a close-up of the entire REIN building. It was surrounded by a seething sea of reaction monitors that swirled and eddied and washed up almost to the entrance and was thrown back again and again. Each wave was met first by cordons of club-wielding, laser-spraying police, then by thousands of civilians who were supporting them.

Overhead, sound cars wheeled and looped like vultures searching for carrion while, in Siskin's voice, their loudspeakers screamed exhortations to the defenders. The policemen and civilians were being reminded that Simulacron-3 was mankind's greatest boon and that on the offensive now were evil powers that would destroy it.

Paralyzing laser beams cut broad swaths of stillness through the attacking forces. But always, behind them, there were more monitors to take the place of the fallen ones. And, even as I watched the action unfold, steady streams of ARM pickup vans descended in the background to discharge reinforcements.

The Reactions building itself was sheathed in an aura of scintillating sparks as projectile guns and brickbats maintained a steady barrage against its repulsion shield.

Vernon Carr hung anxiously in front of the video screen, gesturing aggressively with each assault surge.

"We're going to make it, Avery!" he kept shouting.

Collingsworth and I only stared at each other, our mutual silence an adequate bridge of communication.

I had no interest in the struggle, somehow. Not that it wasn't the most crucial battle ever fought. It was. The very existence of an entire world—a simulectronic universe—hinged on its outcome. For if the reaction monitors won and destroyed Fuller's simulator, the Operator in that Upper Reality would be satisfied and would spare all His creation.

But, perhaps because the stakes were so enormous, I could not bring

120

myself to watch the flow of battle. Or perhaps it was because I knew that, under these circumstances, the Operator would soon couple Himself with Avery. And when that happened it would be the end for both of us.

I wandered over to the door, still open after Carr's entrance, and out into the hall. Numbly, I thumbed the stud to call the elevator.

I stumbled along the staticstrip, back toward the parking lot. I passed the foyer of a building where a public video screen displayed its panorama of violence from the pickup cameras above the Reactions building. But I only turned my head. I didn't *want* to know how the battle was progressing.

A half block from the parking lot I drew up hesitatingly in front of a Psychorama. I stared almost unseeingly at its display posters, which boasted of the current appearance of "The Foremost Abstract Poetrycaster of Our Times—Ragir Rojasta."

A uniformed attendant appealed to the passing pedistrippers, "Come on in, folks. Matinee performance just starting."

My mind was a labyrinth of tortuous, terrified thought. It was halted on a dead-center of stark despair. I had to find some way to clear it so I could decide what to do next—if anything. There was no sense in running. For there was no place to hide. I could be empathy coupled or deprogramed *anywhere*. So I paid my admission and tottered through the foyer.

I took the first empty place I could find in the circular tiers of seats and let my eyes focus indifferently on the central, revolving dais.

Ragir Rojasta sat there, resplendent in his oriental robes and turban, his arms folded, as the rotation of the stage sent his trancelike stare sweeping across the audience. The play of soft lights against his tawny, severe features presented a soothing contrast that invited me to don the Participation Skullcap.

I didn't have to close my eyes to be swept into the essence of Rojasta's conceptualized poetry. Instantly superimposed upon my own field of vision was a great flowing procession of the most dazzling jewels I had ever seen. Rubies and sapphires, diamonds and pearls tumbled over one another, their coruscating beauty blinding even my electrotelepathic appreciation of their elegance.

Against a hazy background of shifting sand and crawling marine life, they sent their brilliant reflections out to strike vivid illumination into murky depths. Then, like the gaping maw of an enormous seadragon, a vacuous hole opened in the ebon distance. And in its depths sparkled the most lustrous gem imaginable.

All around me, as though I weren't in a Psychorama at all, I could feel the wetness of water, the loneliness of desolate, submarine depths, the awful crush of despair and hydrostatic pressure.

Then came the violent, lurching transition—from wetness to blistering dryness, from the suffocating loneliness of unfathomable reaches to the choking aridity of a vast stretch of wasteland.

The only concept that had held its stability during the change had been the incomparable gem. Only, now it, too, was metamorphosing—into a delicate, many-petaled crimson blossom that gave off a poignant redolence.

So hypnotic was Rojasta's projection that I had been sucked irresistibly into the spirit of the reading. And I could now recognize the excerpt:

> *Full many a gem of purest ray serene,*
> *The dark, unfathom'd caves of ocean bear;*
> *Full many a flower is born to blush unseen,*
> *And waste its sweetness on the desert air.*

Gray's *Elegy*, of course.

Now we were looking down on the profuse vegetation flanking one of the Martian canals. The waters roiled with the restless presence of thousands of—

There was a jarring end to the poetrycast as the main lights came up in the Psychorama. A four-sided video screen dropped down to envelop Rojasta and each facet immediately came to life with a picture of the activity outside Reactions, Inc.

Some semblance of order was being restored. The monitors were falling back before the crippling spray from a score of heavy lasers which had been set up on top of the building.

Federal troops had moved in. They were swarming on the roof. They were dropping down by the hundreds in Army vans.

ARM had lost.

The Operator had lost.

The Upper World had failed in its last desperate attempt to destroy Fuller's simulator within the bounds of rational expedient. The Operator couldn't preserve His response-seeking system—our reaction monitors establishment.

I knew what it meant.

This entire world would have to be wiped clean so a new behavior-predicting simulectronic complex could be programed.

I lowered the now dead Participation Skullcap from my head and merely sat there wondering when it would come. Would universal deprograming be effected immediately? Or would the Operator first have to consult a special advisory group, a board of directors?

At least, I consoled myself, I didn't have to worry any longer about being yanked individually, or even being scrutinized through an empathy coupling. If *every* circuit was to be wiped, I would simply go down the drain with all the rest.

Then, just as I had convinced myself that I was no longer a candidate for special treatment by the Operator, it came.

The visual details of the Psychorama blurred and the tiers of seats spun insanely about me. Bending under the crushing impact of faulty empathic coupling, I staggered out into the foyer. The sea that roared in my ears became booming thunder which gradually faded into what sounded like—rumbling laughter!

I cringed against the wall, aware that even now the Operator was picking every bit of vital information from my mind! And the laughter—like a component of nonresonant coupling—became like the beat of a tympanum in my head, sardonic, sadistic.

Then it was gone and my mind was free once more.

I stumbled out onto the staticstrip—just as an air car, with a crescent and star emblazoned on its side, cushioned down onto the street directly in front of me.

"There he is!" the uniformed driver shouted.

And a laser beam, lethal in its pencil-like thinness, lanced out against the side of the building next to my shoulder, crumbling concrete at its focal point.

I spun around and charged back into the foyer.

"Stop, Hall!" someone called out. "You're under arrest for Fuller's murder!"

Was this latest development motivated by Siskin? Had he decided to lower his boom as a final, absolute means of getting me safely out of the way? Or was this a result of programing by the Operator? Was He still sticking to conventional, rational means of disposing of me, despite the fact that He would soon deprogram His entire simulectronic complex?

Two more laser beams lashed out at me before I made it safely back into the Psychorama.

I circled wide around the tiers of seats and plunged out a side exit into the blazing sunlight of the crowded parking lot. Within seconds I was in my car, riding it skyward at full throttle.

✶FOURTEEN✶

THERE WAS NOWHERE TO GO except my cabin on the lake. It was just possible that I might be temporarily safe there if only because it was too obvious a place to hide.

I had no doubt, as I brought the car down into the clearing among needlelike pines and sent it skittering into concealment in the garage, that the police were under orders to shoot to kill. If they were reacting to the tug of Siskin's strings, that was a certainty.

But out here in the forest, I would at least have a chance for concealment and self-defense should a homicide squad cushion down.

On the other hand, if the Operator was pursuing His own purpose of eliminating me, independent of police action, He would follow one of two courses:

Either He would yank me abruptly, without warning—in which case I could do nothing.

Or He would send His agent to handle the job *physically*—to effect the appearance of suicide or accidental death.

And that was what I had wanted all along: a chance to come face-to-face with the Contact Unit. Out here, he would be stripped of his anonymity. He would have to show himself and share with me the isolation of the forest.

I went inside the cabin and selected my heaviest laserifle. Checking its charge, I choked it open to a spread beam. I didn't want to kill the Operator's agent outright. Not when talking with him might suggest a plan of action.

I sat by the window, facing both the lake and clearing, laid the weapon across my legs and waited.

All my reasoning was, of course, predicated on the assumption that, for some purpose, the Simulectronicist Up There was staying His hand on the switch that would wipe out my entire world. Why He might be waiting, I couldn't imagine.

For hours on end, the stillness outside was disturbed only by the furtive movement of wild life among the thickets and up in the foliage, the gentle lapping of the lake upon its rocky shore.

Just after sundown, I went into the kitchen and broke open a pack of camp-out rations. Afraid to turn on any lights, I sat huddled beneath one of the windows and went through the mechanical motions of eating. And all the while I couldn't dismiss the incongruity implicit in the need of an immaterial being for immaterial food.

It was almost dark when I returned to the trophy room, drew the curtain, and tuned in the evening videocast. I adjusted the volume to a whisper.

On the screen was a picture of the debris-strewn street in front of Reactions, Inc. Close-ups of federal troops outside the building were shown next, while the announcer deplored the "bloodshed and violence that have taken their toll on this gruesome day."

"But," he went on soberly, "rioting is not the only development that brings Horace P. Siskin's latest enterprise boldly into the news this evening.

"There is more—much more. There is intrigue and conspiracy. Murder and—a fugitive. All are directly involved in the alleged Association of Reactions Monitors' plot to deprive an anxious world of the blessings that will flow from Horace Siskin's simulator."

My own image leaped onto the screen and was identified by the announcer.

"This is the man," he said, "who is wanted for the murder of Hannon J. Fuller, former technical director at Reactions. He is the man whom Siskin trusted implicitly. Into Douglas Hall's hands was placed the profound obligation of perfecting the simulator after Fuller's supposedly accidental death.

"But, police charged today, Fuller was actually *murdered* by Hall for personal gain. And when Hall saw he was going to be denied that gain he turned treacherously on the Siskin Establishment, on the simulator itself.

"For Douglas Hall is the man who was trailed this morning by Siskin's own security forces as he entered ARM headquarters to seal his treachery. He did that by perpetrating the unsuccessful mass attack on REIN."

I tensed. Siskin, then, had known instantly about my visit to the pollsters' headquarters. And he had assumed I was planning to betray his conspiracy with the party. So he had hit his panic button and dispatched the police with shoot-to-kill orders.

And suddenly I recognized one possible reason why the Operator hadn't yanked me yet: He might have seen that Siskin was, unwittingly and in pursuit of his own objectives, *taking care of the job for Him!*

Oh, the Operator could help out a bit. For instance, if it appeared the law was dragging its heels, He might pull off another empathic coupling, find where I was hiding, then program the police to conceive of looking for me at the cabin.

He would either arrange it *that* way, or He would send His Contact Unit to do the job. It was a cinch He wasn't merely going to yank me, and then have to reorient a whole cast of ID characters to the alternate fact that I had never existed.

But even as I tried to surmise the Operator's strategy, I realized finally that the entire world *might not be erased after all!* Perhaps the Operator had decided to iron out the present complications, then have another—an absolutely final—try at eliminating Fuller's simulator.

The videocaster was still on the subject of my supposed treachery:

"Hall's heinous activities, however, didn't end with his alleged murder of Hannon J. Fuller and his purported betrayal of Siskin and the simulator—not as far as the police are concerned."

A picture of Collingsworth flashed on the screen.

"For," the announcer lowered his voice to a grave pitch, "he is additionally sought in connection with the most ghastly murder in local police annals—that of Avery Collingsworth, consultant psychologist on Reactions' staff."

It was a full minute before I took another breath. The Operator had *already* gotten around to Avery!

The newscaster went on to describe the "stark brutality" of Dr. Collingsworth's murder.

"Police," he intoned emotionally, "called the death the most vicious mutilation ever committed. Dismembered fragments of the body—joints of fingers, forearms, ears—were found strewn about Collingsworth's study. Each stump was, in turn, carefully cauterized to control loss of blood so that death would be forestalled during the barbarous torture."

Appalled, I snapped off the video set. I tried to shake my head clear, but I could see only visions of Avery—helpless, terrified, knowing all the while that he couldn't escape what was happening to him.

It hadn't been a physical agent, a Contact Unit, who had done that. It had been the Operator Himself, using extra-physical means of torture. I could see Collingsworth screaming in agony while the terminal segment of his little finger was detached, as though severed by a knife; while a modified laser beam appeared from nowhere to seal off the stub.

I rose, swearing in horror. I knew now that the Operator *was* a sadist. Perhaps, in that Higher Existence, everybody was.

I went back to the window, opened the curtains on the murky purple of late twilight and sat there gripping my rifle and waiting. For what? The police? The Contact Unit?

Briefly, it occurred to me that the Operator might not know where I was. But I rejected that possibility. He had probably already coupled himself with me since my arrival here. Oh, that was possible, all right—even likely. For I saw now that I had been aware of previous couplings only because He had wanted it that way—so He could savor my tortured reaction.

Outside, the dark deepened and a myriad stars, swept into and out of visibility by wind-tossed foliage, made the blackness seem like a lambent field of fireflies. Crickets chirruped their doleful accompaniment to the flickering night. In the distance, a bullfrog rounded out the score with an occasional bass note.

The illusion of reality was oh, *so* complete. Even the minor details had been meticulously provided. Up There, They had stinted on but few of Their simulectronic props. They had inadvertently allowed only minor, imperceptible inconsistencies.

I found myself looking into my star-spangled sky, trying to see through the universal illusion into absolute reality. But, then, that Real

World was in no *physical* direction from my own. It was not in my universe, nor I in Its. At the same time, though, It was everywhere around me, hidden by an electronic veil.

I tried to imagine how Phil Ashton had felt when he had climbed up out of Fuller's simulator. My thoughts wandered up a notch to the Higher Existence. What must it be like Up There? How vastly different from the pseudoreality I knew?

Then I understood that it *couldn't* be very different at all. The world of Phil Ashton, sustained by the currents in Fuller's simulator, had had to be, in effect, a replica of my own if the predictions we got from that analog creation were to have valid application up here.

Similarly, my world would have to track that Higher Existence. Most of the institutions would have to be the same. Our culture, our historical background, even our heritage and destiny would have to correspond.

And the Operator, and all the other people Up There, would have to be human beings, just like us, since our existence could be justified only as analogs of Them.

The darkness outside faded before a cast of intensifying illumination that was playing against the trees. Then I heard the swish of an air car as it followed its lights down.

I studded the door open and hurled myself outside, diving behind a hedge and bringing my rifle up before me.

The car cushioned down, extinguished its lights and cut its engine. Desperately, I squinted into the suddenly impenetrable night.

It *wasn't* a police car. And there was only one occupant.

The door opened and the driver climbed halfway out.

I cut loose with the laserifle.

Secondary illumination from the broad crimson beam limned the features of—*Jinx Fuller!* And, in that same confusing moment, I watched her slump to the ground.

Shouting her name, I hurled the rifle aside and lunged into the clearing, boundlessly grateful that I had choked the weapon down to only stun intensity.

Long after midnight I was still pacing in the cabin, waiting for her to revive. But I knew she would be unconscious for some time, since her head had been included in the laser spraying. Nevertheless, she would suffer but few after-effects, thanks to the broad beam.

Innumerable times during the early morning hours I groped through the darkness to place cold towels on her head. But it wasn't until dawn began filtering through the curtains that she moaned and brought a limp hand to her forehead.

She opened her eyes and smiled. "What happened?"

"I sprayed you, Jinx," I said, contritely. "I didn't mean to. I thought you were the Con—the police."

I had caught myself just in time. I couldn't complicate things further by re-exposing her to bits of forbidden knowledge.

She tried to sit up. I supported the effort with a hand behind her back.

"I—I heard about the trouble you were in," she said. "I had to come."

"You shouldn't have! No telling what might happen. You've got to leave!"

Attempting to stand, she only fell back upon the couch. She wouldn't be able to go anywhere for a while—not by herself.

"No, Doug," she insisted. "I want to stay *here* with you. I came as soon as I found out."

With my help she finally made it to her feet and clung to me, crying softly against my cheek. I held her as though she might be the only real thing in this entire illusive world. And I staggered under an overwhelming sense of loss. All my life I had wanted someone like Jinx. Finding her, however, had been but a hollow accomplishment. For there was no reality save the surge of biasing impulses in simulectronic circuits.

She backed off and stared compassionately into my face, then came forward again. She pressed her lips against mine, fiercely. It was almost as though she, too, knew what was going to happen.

While I kissed her I thought wistfully of what might have been. If only the Operator had succeeded in having Fuller's simulator destroyed! If only I were still with Reactions, so I could do it myself! If only the Simulectronicist in that Upper Reality had reoriented me as he had reoriented Jinx!

"We're going to stay together, Doug," she whispered. "I'm never going to leave you, darling."

"But you can't!" I protested.

Hadn't she realized how impossible everything was? On the basis of the threat posed by Siskin and his police, alone, there was no hope for me.

Then I drew back confused, forced once again to consider reasonable alternatives. Either her love for me was so limitless that nothing would stand in its way. Or she simply wasn't aware of all the police charges against me. Certainly she hadn't heard *how* Collingsworth had died, or she wouldn't be here now.

"You know I'm wanted for the murder of your father, don't you?" I said.

"You didn't do it, darling."

"And—Avery Collingsworth?"

She hesitated. "You didn't—couldn't have—done that."

It was almost as though she were speaking from personal, absolute knowledge. Her loyalty, her love were that intense. I was only thankful now that They *had* successfully reoriented her, that she didn't have to face the peril I was now facing.

She caught my hand and turned toward the door. "Maybe we can get away, Doug! We'll find some place to hide!"

When I didn't move, she relaxed her grip and my hand fell from hers.

"No," she told herself despondently, "there's *nowhere* we can go. They'll find us."

She didn't know how true that was. And I was infinitely relieved that she was altogether unaware of the ambiguity of the "they" she had used.

There was a noise outside and I seized my rifle. At the window, I parted the curtains, but saw only a doe thrashing through the hedge to get to the now-empty feeding bin.

Alertly, it lifted its head and looked toward the cabin. My fears allayed, I let the curtains fall back in place. Then I tensed. Rarely were there deer in the area at this time of the year. I turned back to the window. The animal headed toward Jinx's car, stopped a short distance away and regarded the open door.

I tightened my grip on the laserifle. The deer in this lower world might be simple props, existing only as shadows cast against the illusive background to add to the appearance of reality. But, then again, they might enjoy as much pseudo-physiological validity, in a limited sense, as the ID units themselves.

If the latter were the case, there was no reason why a doe couldn't be conveniently programed to wander into a clearing before a lakeside cabin and, through empathy coupling, monitor what was going on in the vicinity!

The animal turned its head toward the cabin, ears perking at the still brightening sky and nose twitching.

"What is it?" Jinx asked.

"Nothing," I said, concealing my anxiety. "If you feel up to it, you might dial us a couple of cups of coffee."

I watched her stagger toward the kitchen, then eased the window open, just wide enough to accommodate the linear intensifier of the weapon. I choked down a bit on the spread.

Eventually the doe turned away, heading for the garage.

I hit the firing stud and sprayed the animal for a full ten seconds, concentrating on its head as it lay motionless.

At the hissing sound of the discharge, Jinx was back in the kitchen doorway. "Doug! It's not—"

"No. Just a deer. I dropped it for a couple of hours. It was about to get into your car."

We sipped coffee silently, across the bar from each other in the kitchen. Her face was drawn, stripped of its cosmetic propriety, tense. An errant tress of dark hair hung down to eclipse part of an eye. But her appearance could not be described as haggard. For in the absence of the sheen of sophistication, the charm of her youth came through, unpretentious, unspoiled.

She glanced at her watch, for the second time since accepting the cups from the slot, and reached across the bar to take both my hands. "What are we going to do, darling?"

I lied with profound intensity. "I only have to stay hidden for a day or two. Then everything will work itself out." I paused to improvise further. "You see, Whitney can prove I didn't kill Collingsworth. He's probably doing that right now."

She didn't appear relieved. She only looked down at her watch again.

"That's why you're going to get in that car and cushion off just as soon as you feel strong enough," I continued. "If you turn up missing too, that may double their chance of finding me. They might even think of looking out here."

Stubbornly, she said, "I'm staying with you."

Not feeling like arguing the point at the moment, I trusted in my ability to persuade her later on. "Hold down the fort. I'm going to shave while I still have the chance."

When I had finished ten minutes later, I stepped back into the trophy room and found the front door open. Jinx was out there bending over the stunned doe. She glanced back at the cabin and continued casually across the clearing.

I watched her disappear into the forest, carrying herself with the graceful, flowing motions of a nymph. Even though I was determined she would leave as soon as possible, I was glad she had come.

Then a laser beam of mocking realization exploded against my consciousness: *How had she known I was at the cabin?* I had never told her about this place.

I grabbed my rifle and started after her. Sprinting across the clearing, I plunged into the woods. Among the giant, swaying pines, I paused and strained for the sound of feet crunching on fallen needles to determine which way she had gone.

Then I heard what I was listening for and charged off in that direction. I broke through underbrush into a small clearing and pulled up—face-to-face with a startled ten-point buck.

Beyond, far beyond, I saw Jinx poised in a slanted shaft of early sunlight. But inconsistency sounded an alarm and I stared back at the buck. Though startled, it hadn't bolted.

Abruptly, the instant, fierce pressures of faulty empathic coupling burst upon my senses. Stunned from the impact of roaring noise and vertiginous disorientation, I dropped my rifle.

Through the inner bedlam, I was again aware of what sounded like savage laughter flowing along the simulectronic bond that now joined all my faculties with those of the Operator.

Rearing up, the buck clawed air with its forehoofs, then dropped back down. It lowered its head and charged.

I staggered under the ordeal of dissonant coupling, but managed to pull myself partly out of the way of the onrushing deer.

An antler ripped my shirt sleeve and sliced through my forearm like a wire-thin laser beam. And I imagined that, in response, the laughter of the Operator rose to an almost hysterical pitch.

Again the buck reared and I tried to twist out from under descending hoofs. I almost made it. But the full force of the animal's weight pounded down upon my shoulder and sent me sprawling.

When I rolled over and came up again, however, it was with the rifle in my hand. I cut the deer down in the middle of its next charge. And, almost in the same moment, I was freed from coupling.

Up ahead, Jinx was still standing in the shaft of sunlight, unaware of what had happened behind her.

But even as I watched, she glanced upward expectantly, then vanished.

✶FIFTEEN✶

FOR AN ETERNITY, I STOOD frozen in the clearing, the stunned buck at my feet, my eyes locked on the spot where Jinx had disappeared.

Now I knew *she* was the Contact Unit. I had been so wrong in my interpretation of her actions. I had thought she had learned, as Fuller's daughter, the details of his "basic discovery" but had been trying to hide them from me so that I wouldn't be deprogramed.

Upon her disappearance from her house, I had imagined she had been temporarily yanked in order to have the forbidden knowledge stricken from her circuits. I had been certain, later, that erasure of that data had allowed her love for me to find full expression.

But it hadn't been that way at all.

She had acted odd, before her first disappearance, because she and the Simulectronicist Up There had been concerned. They were worried that I would learn Fuller's secret.

Then Collingsworth, programed to dissuade me from my forbidden convictions, succeeded in making me believe I had been suffering such an unlikely thing as "pseudoparanoia." That belief was uppermost in my thoughts the night I had been empathy-coupled while in the restaurant with Jinx.

The Operator assumed then that I had been thrown off the track. And Jinx, as a Contact Unit, had begun playing the role of ardent lover in order to lure me further from my suspicions.

That was the way things had rocked along until yesterday, when the Operator had learned from Collingsworth that not only I, but Avery

135

too, stubbornly doubted that our world was real. And Jinx had come here last night for only one purpose: to keep me under her thumb until arrangements could be made for my "natural" death. Maybe she was going to "kill" me herself!

Eventually I was aware of warm blood from the wound dripping off my fingertips. I tore the shirt sleeve off and wrapped it tightly about my gored forearm. Then I started back for the cabin.

I tried again, but couldn't budge the inconsistencies. For instance, how could Jinx—just disappear? None of the ID characters in Fuller's simulator could do that, unless—

But, of course! Whenever I withdrew after projecting myself down into Simulacron-3 on a direct surveillance circuit, I did *just* that!

Jinx, then, was neither a Contact Unit nor a reactional entity. *She was a projection of some physical person in that Upper Reality!*

But still there were inconsistencies. Why hadn't *I* simply been re-oriented, as had other ID units, to the alternate fact that Lynch had never existed?

Moreover, the Operator must have frequently coupled Himself empathically with Collingsworth in order to program him in the campaign to destroy Fuller's simulator. Why, then, had He not learned from Avery, earlier than yesterday, that I could not be shaken from my convictions on the true nature of reality?

The swishing, crackling sound of a falling tree jolted me from my thoughts. Startled, I glanced up.

A huge pine was toppling right overhead!

I tried frantically to get out of the way, but it hit the ground with jarring impact, its upper foliage lashing out at me. Bowled over, I was hurled against another trunk.

Confounded, I rose and backed off, fingering the raw furrow one of the branches had raked in my cheek. Then suddenly my head was reverberating again with the derisive, sickening effects of faulty coupling.

I raced for the cabin, desperately trying to suppress the relentless pain of dissonant empathy. I reached the edge of the clearing, head pounding, vision dazed. And I drew up sharply.

A massive black bear was sniffing Jinx's car. It sensed my presence and turned. But I wasn't going to take any chances. I killed it with a pencil-thin laser beam.

That must have deprived the Operator of an eagerly anticipated bonus of sadistic appreciation. For, as the animal dropped, the bond of empathy broke and I was relieved of its fierce pressure.

But it was clear now that I had to get away from the forest. Here there were too many elements of nature that could be manipulated against me. If I had any chance at all, it would be back in the city, where the Operator might not be as free to program my counterfeit environment against me.

In the cabin, I lost no time dressing my arm wound and applying balm to the stinging laceration that ran from my temple to my jaw.

Through the fog of fear and desperation, however, I was somehow able to think about Jinx. Had there ever actually been a Jinx Fuller in my world? Or had she all along been but a projection?

I reached for my coat, tasting at last the bitter irony of having fallen in love with her. I, but a ripple of illusion; she, a real, tangible person. I could imagine her mocking laughter, joining exuberantly with that of the Operator.

Suddenly doubtful, I paused in the doorway. Back to the city? Where Siskin's police were out to shoot me down? Where, even if I should elude them, they had a sadistic Ally Up There all too eager to program them in the right direction?

There was a blur of movement in the corner of my vision and I ducked reflexively under a flurry of wings and a raucous *caw-caw*.

But the crow had not purposely aimed itself at me. Confounded, I turned and watched it bank and fly straight into the kitchen. Curiosity exceeded apprehension and I went back inside. The bird had landed on the floor and was pecking at the stud on the door of the packaged power unit compartment.

I thought of the exposed leads within. And, for a horrifying moment of indecision, I was rooted in the cabin.

Then I charged outside, racing halfway across the clearing before I hurled myself to the ground. The cabin went up in a shattering roar, spewing debris over an acre of forest and taking the garage along with it.

Fortunately, none of the hurtling stone and timber struck either me or Jinx's car in the center of the clearing—a development of which I should have been immediately suspicious.

Surveying the wreckage, I was convinced at last that I would have to take my chances in the city.

At two thousand feet over the forest, the main power supply failed. I switched to emergency and the vanes began spinning again. But the engine coughed spasmodically and with each sputter the car plunged another hundred feet.

I fought the wheel frantically to retain some degree of control. Finally I managed to kick the craft around toward the lake, hoping there would be a final burst of power to cushion the impact.

Just then the Operator cut in once more on my perceptive faculties. The torment of faulty coupling was less unbearable this time, however. It could only be that my plight was providing Him with sufficient delight in itself.

Abruptly a strong headwind began churning the surface of the lake into a frothing mantle and my angle of descent became more precipitous. I was going to crash into the trees before I broke over the shore line!

But an unexpected burst of power boosted me over the hump and another cushioned the car just five feet above the lashing waves.

Knuckles whitened by my fierce grip on the wheel, I sat there trembling and perspiring, as the vehicle climbed back into the sky.

I could sense the Operator's ecstatic reaction. And I knew, from the intensity of His emotional response, that I was not going to be let off that easily. Bracing myself, I waited for whatever would come next as the car, still gaining altitude, continued on toward the city.

With Fuller's simulator, I remembered, coupling could be modified to permit reciprocal empathy. That device would be used, for instance, whenever I wanted to communicate with Phil Ashton without having to project myself into his world.

So I tried to reach back across the empathic bond, realizing all the while that He would be aware of my intention. But I could perceive nothing through His senses. It was a one-way coupling. Yet I could almost sense His presence. It was as though I could get the "feel" of Him. And vivid was the impression I received of malicious, twisted purpose.

Then I frowned, perplexed. There was the profound suggestion that the bond existing between us was one of more than just empathy. There seemed to be the obscure hint of a certain similarity between the two of us. Physical? In character? Or was it merely reflective of our analogous circumstances—each a simulectronicist in his own world?

Without further interference from the Operator, I leveled off at six thousand feet. Then I tilted the car's nose down, exchanging lift for thrust, and sped for the city. The concrete-glass hulk of the metropolis spread out before me, only a few miles away.

Would I make it? Then I sank despondently back in the seat. Did I *want* to make it? Out there in the forest, alone with the Operator and all His hostile nature, I had little chance of survival. On the other hand, in the city there would be no animals available for attack programing. But what about the *inanimate* things? The lashing belt of a suddenly snapped high-speed pedistrip? A falling cornice? An air car out of control?

Anxiously, I stared through the plexidome at a small, gray cloud that bisected the horizon. It grew alarmingly as the car carried me directly toward it. I tried to steer clear, but too late.

In the next instant I was in a swirling, darting flight of—redwinged blackbirds? At *six thousand* feet? They thudded against the car, spattering its plexidome. They were sucked in by the hundreds through the dorsal intakes. The vanes groaned and chugged against the almost solid mass, taking a terrific pounding. The powerplant coughed and wheezed, froze, then freed itself—only to repeat the ominous cycle.

Plunging down, I winced as the Operator switched in anew on my senses. Again, the empathic coupling was bearable. And once more I labored under the incongruous impression that the person who was battening on my desperation and fear bore a certain incomprehensible similarity to me.

The battered vanes, trying valiantly to check the drop, began vibrating. The shudder intensified and presently it seemed that the craft was going to shake itself apart. Then the dome cracked, shattered, and went flying past my head. I glanced outside to see how far I was from the ground. And, ironically, I perceived that I was plunging almost straight toward the low, broad building that was Reactions, Inc.

I had so little altitude now that I could even see the troops. And I wondered whether the Operator, in a brilliant stroke of strategy, was going to send me crashing into the building to wipe out both myself and Fuller's machine at the same time.

If that had been his plan, however, he had forgotten about the emergency net protecting the city. For, with the car scarcely two hundred feet above the building, three intensely yellow beams leaped up from the surface and converged on the helpless craft.

They absorbed its momentum. Pivoting slowly and in perfect coordination, they moved me along several hundred feet above the surface toward the nearest emergency receiving station.

But the Upper Simulectronicist wasn't going to be deprived of yet another brutal flourish. The car's powerplant burst into flames filling the cab with fierce heat. I had no choice. Still a hundred feet above the receiving area, I dived from the craft.

By then the Operator had broken empathy. Otherwise, he might easily have arranged for me to slip out of the receiving beam. But as it was, I stayed safely within the brilliant cone and was lowered to the apron several seconds ahead of the car.

I didn't waste any time there—not with traffic police and firemen spilling out of the station. Leaping from the apron, I hurdled the staticstrip and landed upon the slowest pedibelt. Within a moment I had worked my way to the highspeed conveyor.

Two blocks away, I returned to the staticstrip and walked as casually as I could into the nearest hotel.

In the lobby, an automatic news vendor was headlining the day's developments in an impersonal, soft voice:

"Siskin Schedules Public Demonstration of Simulacron-3 Tomorrow Morning! Machine to Solve First Problem in Human Relations!"

But Siskin's strategy held little interest for me as I took the belt to the rear of the lobby and found an obscure pair of chairs half concealed by a huge wax plant. Haggard and insensitive, I dropped into the nearer of the two.

"Doug! Oh, Doug—wake up!"

Somehow, exhaustion must have brought sleep. But I swam wearily back toward consciousness, aware first of the tingling numbness in my spent legs. Then I opened my eyes and saw Jinx seated in the adjacent chair. I started and she placed her hand on my arm.

Wincing, I sprang up and tried to bolt back toward the crowded part of the lobby. But my legs buckled and I almost fell. I stood there swaying and trembling, trying frantically to place one foot in front of the other.

She rose and shoved me back into the chair. Confounded, I glanced down at my legs.

"Yes, Doug," she said. "I sprayed them—so you wouldn't be able to run from me."

Now I could see the bulge of the small laser gun in her purse.

"I know—everything," I blurted out. "You're not one of us! You're not even an ID unit!"

There was no surprise on her face, only a pained uneasiness.

"That's right," she said softly. "And now I'm aware of how much you know. But I wasn't an hour ago, when we were back there at the cabin. That's why I withdrew in the forest. I had to find out how much you had figured out for yourself—or how much he had *let* you figure out"

"He? Who?"

"The Operator."

"There *is* an Operator, then? This *is* a simulectronic world?"

She didn't say anything.

"And you're just a—a projection?" I asked.

"Just a projection." She dropped back into the chair.

I think I would have felt less despondent if she had denied it. However, she only sat there grim-faced, offering no hope, giving me time to realize fully that I *was* merely a reactional unit. Whereas she was a real, material person whom I could perceive only in an ingenious reflection of her true self.

She leaned toward me. "But you're wrong, Doug! I'm *not* trying to trick you. I only want to help."

I touched my lacerated cheek, glanced down at my laser-sprayed legs. But she didn't interpret the gesture in the same sarcastic vein I had intended it. Instead she said:

"When I withdrew this morning, it was because I wanted to run a spot empathy check on you. I had to see just how much you did suspect. That was so I would know just where to start in on what I had to tell you."

She laid her hand on my arm and, again, I shrank away.

"You've been almost completely wrong about me," she continued defensively. "At first I was desperate as I watched you work toward the knowledge you weren't supposed to have."

"Knowledge forbidden all ID units?"

"Yes. I tried my best to keep it from you. Naturally, I destroyed the notes in Dr. Fuller's study—physically. But that was a mistake. It only made you more suspicious. Instead, we should have removed the evidence through simulectronic reprograming. But, at the time, we were too busy manipulating the reaction monitors to call their strike."

She glanced down the lobby. "I even programed a pollster to scare you off by warning you on the street that morning."

"Collingsworth too? You made him try to talk me out of it?"

"No. The Operator was responsible for that strategy."

Did she want me to believe she had had no part in Avery's brutal murder?

"Oh, Doug! I tried so many ways to make you forget about Fuller's death, about Lynch, about your suspicions. But that night when you took me to the restaurant I was ready to admit failure."

"But I *told* you then that I was convinced it had all been merely my imagination."

"Yes, I know. Only, I didn't believe you. I thought you were just trying to trick me. But when I withdrew from direct projection later that night the Operator told me he had just checked you. He said you *were* finally sold on the idea of pseudoparanoia and that now we could concentrate on destroying Fuller's simulator.

"Oh I learned, when I spoke with you over the videophone the next day, that you had come into the house after my withdrawal. But I passed it off lightly and you seemed to accept my explanation. At least you didn't do anything afterward to make me suspicious."

I squirmed away from her. "And you spread it on thick, hoping you would keep me off the track."

She glanced down at her hands. "I suppose you have every right to look at it that way. But that isn't true."

She appeared to be wrestling with the choice of proving she hadn't simply been manipulating me. But, instead, she said:

"Then, when everything started happening to you yesterday, I knew things had gone wrong. My first reaction was to rush out to where you were as soon as possible. But when I got there I realized I hadn't acted wisely. I hadn't foreseen how difficult it would be talking to you like this, without knowing how much you suspected, what you thought of me.

"So, the first chance I got, I withdrew again and cut in on you through a direct empathy circuit. Oh it wasn't easy, Doug. The Operator had been in almost constant contact with you. I had to take a parallel circuit. I had to switch in with the greatest of care—so he wouldn't realize what I was doing.

"But when I did, I saw everything—instantly. I hadn't *dreamed*— Oh, Doug, he's so vicious, so inhuman!"

"The Operator?"

She lowered her head, as though embarrassed. "I knew he was something like that. But I didn't realize how far he had gone. I didn't know that, for the most part, he was just toying with you for the malicious pleasure he could get out of it."

Once again she glanced down the lobby.

"What are you looking for?" I asked bluntly.

She turned back toward me. "The police. He may have programed them to the fact that you returned to the city."

Then I saw it all. Now I *knew* what her purpose was in sitting here and talking with me.

I grabbed for her purse, but she sprang from the chair.

I struggled to my leaden feet and staggered after her.

"No, no—Doug! You don't understand!"

"I understand, all right!" I swore at my legs because they could hardly support my weight. "You're just trying to keep me pinned down until the Operator *can* steer the police to me!"

"No! That's not true! You've got to believe me!"

I managed to maneuver her into a corner and started to close in.

But she drew the laser gun and sprayed my arms and chest. She narrowed its beam and raked my throat. She opened it to its widest dispersion and caught me lightly across the head.

I only stood there swaying like a drunk, eyes half closed, thoughts mired.

She put the gun away, took my limp arm and draped it about her neck. She supported me around the waist and struggled toward the elevator.

An elderly couple passed us and the man smiled at Jinx while the woman cast us a disparaging glance.

Jinx smiled back and said, "Oh, these conventions!"

On the fifteenth floor, she struggled under my almost dead weight to the first door on the left. Its lock responded to her biocapacitance and she walked me in.

"I got this room just before I woke you up in the lobby," she explained. "I didn't imagine this would be easy."

She let me fall across the bed, then straightened and stared down at me. And I wondered what was behind the impassive expression that clung to her attractive features. Triumph? Pity? Uncertainty?

She drew the gun again, set it for a slightly narrower beam and aimed it at my head. "We don't have to worry about the Operator for a while. Thank God he has to rest *some* time. And rest is what you need, too."

Unwavering, she pressed the firing stud.

⋆SIXTEEN⋆

WHEN I AWOKE, THE DARKNESS in the room was but a feeble barrier against the blazing lights of the city that poured in through the windows. I lay still, intent upon not letting her know I was conscious until I could determine where she was. Imperceptibly, I shifted an arm, then a leg. There was no suggestion of lingering pain. At least it had been a careful spraying, which had left few after-effects.

There was movement on the chair near the bed. If only I could turn my head unobtrusively in her direction, I might learn where the laser gun was.

But, as I lay there, I realized I had been asleep at least ten hours. And nothing had happened. Siskin's police hadn't come. The Operator hadn't yanked me. And, more significantly, Jinx *hadn't* given me a lethal spraying here in the seclusion of the hotel room, which certainly would have been the easiest way of obliterating me.

"You're awake, aren't you?" Her clear words cut into the room's subdued light.

I turned over and sat up.

She rose, raised her hand into the capacitance-sensing range of the ceiling switch and the lights came on. She waved them to a soft intensity, then came over to the bed.

"Feel better now?"

I said nothing.

"I know how bewildered and frightened you must be." She sat beside me. "I am too. That's why we shouldn't be working against each other."

145

I scanned the room.

"The laser gun's over there." She indicated the arm of the chair. Then, as though to demonstrate her sincerity, she reached over and offered it to me.

Perhaps, after sleeping off my exhaustion, I was more inclined to trust her. But I could do that as well with the gun in my pocket as with it in her possession. I took it from her outstretched hand.

She walked over to the window and stared into the artificially illuminated night. "He'll let you alone until morning."

Standing uncertainly, I tested my legs. No numbness. There was no trace of the spraying, not even the dull headache that sometimes follows.

She turned toward me. "Hungry?"

I nodded.

She went over to the delivery slot and studded the door open. She brought the self-heating tray over and set it on a chair beside the bed.

I tried a few mouthfuls, then said, "Evidently you want me to believe you're helping me."

She closed her eyes hopelessly. "Yes. But there really isn't much I can do."

"Who are you?"

"Jinx. No, not Jinx Fuller. Another one. It doesn't matter. Names aren't important."

"What happened to Jinx Fuller?"

"She never existed. Not until a few weeks ago." She nodded cognizantly before I could protest. "Sure—you've known her for years. But that knowledge is just the effects of retroprograming. You see, two things happened at the same time. Dr. Fuller reasoned out the true nature of his world. And, up there, we recognized Fuller's simulator as a complication that must be eliminated. So we decided to plant an observer down here to keep close watch on developments."

"We? Meaning—who?"

She elevated her eyes briefly. "The simulectronic engineers. I was selected as the observer. Through retroprograming, we created the further illusion that Fuller had had a daughter."

"But I remember her as a child!"

"*Everybody*—every relevant reactor—remembers her as a child. That was the only way we could justify my presence down here."

146

I took some more food.

She glanced out the window. "It won't be morning for a few hours yet. We'll be safe until then."

"Why?"

"Even the Operator can't stay at it twenty-four hours a day. This world is on a time-equivalent basis with the real one."

No matter how I reasoned it out, she *had* to be here for one of two purposes: to help the Operator destroy Fuller's simulator, or to effect my own elimination. There was no other possibility. For I could imagine myself in an analogous capacity—descending into the counterfeit world of *Fuller's* simulator. Down there, I would consider myself a projection of a real person, in contrast to the purely analog characters around me. And it would be impossible for me to become concerned with the insignificant affairs of any of those lower ID units.

"What *is* your purpose here?" I asked frankly.

"I want to be with you, darling."

Darling? How naive did she think I was? Was I supposed to believe a *real* person might actually be in love with a reactional unit—*a simulectronic shadow?*

Apparently distraught, she placed tense fingers before her mouth. "Oh, Doug—you don't know how savage the Operator is!"

"Yes I do," I said bitterly.

"I didn't realize what he was doing until I coupled myself with you yesterday. Then I saw what he had been up to. You see, he has absolute authority over his simulator, over this world. It's sort of like being a god, I suppose. At least, he must have eventually begun looking at it that way."

She paused and stared at the floor. "I guess he was sincere at first in trying to program the destruction of Fuller's simulator. He had to be, because if Fuller's machine succeeded, there wouldn't be any room down here for our response-seeking system—the reaction monitors. He was also sincere, I imagine, about humanely doing away with any reactor who became aware of his simulectronic nature.

"When you stepped out of line, he tried to kill you—quickly, clinically. But something happened. I suppose he realized how much pleasure he was getting from putting you through your paces. And suddenly he didn't *want* to do away with you—not too quickly, anyway."

147

I broke in thoughtfully. "Collingsworth said he could understand how simulectronicists might think of themselves as gods."

She stared intensely at me. "And, remember: when Collingsworth spoke with you, he had been programed by the Operator to say just that."

I took another few mouthfuls and shoved the tray aside.

"It wasn't until yesterday," she went on, "that I realized he could have solved his problem, as far as you were concerned, any time he wanted, simply by reorienting you. But no. There was too much perverted gratification to be had by letting you come close to Fuller's secret, then pushing you away, steering you all the while toward some such fate as he arranged for Collingsworth."

I stiffened. "You don't think he'd try mutilating—"

"I don't know. There's no telling what he'll do. That's why I've got to stay down here with you."

"What can *you* do?"

"Perhaps nothing. We can only wait and see."

Anxiously, she put her arms around me. Did she expect me to think that, just because someone up there had singled me out for torture, she wanted to be with me in a spirit of compassion? Well, I could pull the pedistrip out from under her pretense easily enough.

"Jinx, you're a—material person. I'm just a figment of somebody's imagination. You *can't* be in love with me!"

She stepped back, apparently hurt. "Oh, but I am, Doug! It's—so difficult to explain."

I had imagined it would be. She sat on the edge of the bed and faced me uncertainly. Her eyes were restless. Of course she was at a loss to explain how she could love me under the circumstances.

I ran my hand into my pocket and fingered the laser gun. I made certain its setting was for full spread. Then I whipped it out and turned suddenly on her.

Eyes widening, she started to rise. "No, Doug—don't!"

I gave her a superficial spraying, focusing on her head, and she fell back unconscious across the bed. The short burst would hold her for at least an hour.

Meanwhile I could move around and think, free from the pressure of her presence. And almost immediately I saw what I should do next.

148

Considering the plan, I took my time washing, then using the lavatory's autoshaver. At the personal dispenser, I dialed in my size and waited for the plastic-wrapped, throw-away shirt to appear.

Finally refreshed, I checked the time. It was well after midnight. I went back and looked down at Jinx. I placed the laser gun on the pillow and knelt beside the bed.

Her dark hair was satiny and lustrous as it flared out on the spread. I buried my hands in its soft depths, sending my fingers groping over her scalp. Finally I located the sagittal suture and explored back, pressing firmly in all the while, until I found the minute depression I was searching for.

Holding my finger over the spot, I set the laser gun at the required focus, then placed its intensifier exactly where my finger had been. I hit the stud briefly, then once again for good measure.

It struck me momentarily as being irrational, my performing a *physical* action on an intangible projection. But the illusion of reality was, had to be, so complete that all pseudo-physical causes were properly translated into analogous simulectronic effects. Projections were no exception.

I stepped back. *Now* let her try deception! With her volitional center well sprayed, I could believe anything she'd say, for the next several hours at least.

I bent over her. "Jinx, can you hear me?"

Without opening her eyes, she nodded.

"You're not to withdraw," I ordered. "Do you understand? You're not to withdraw until *I say so*."

She nodded again.

Fifteen minutes later, she began awakening.

I paced in front of her as she sat there on the bed, somewhat groggy from the latter laser treatment. Her eyes, though distant, were clear and steady.

"Up," I said.

And she stood.

"Down."

She sat obediently.

It was clear I had zeroed in on her volitional center.

I fired the first question. "How much of what you just told me is false?"

Her eyes remained focused on nothing. Her expression was frozen. "None of it."

I started. There I was, stumped at the very beginning. But it *couldn't* all have been true!

Thinking back to the first time I had seen her, I asked, "Do you remember the drawing of Achilles and the tortoise?"

"Yes."

"But you denied later there *was* such a drawing."

She said nothing. Then I knew why she was silent. I hadn't asked a question or directed her to make a statement. "Did you later deny there was such a drawing?"

"Yes."

"Why?"

"Because I was supposed to throw you off the track, block you from vital knowledge."

"Because that was what the Operator wanted?"

"Only partly."

"Why else?"

"Because I was falling in love with you and didn't want to see you get involved in dangerous circumstances."

Again I was stymied. For I knew it was as impossible for her to feel genuine affection toward me as it would be for me to become amorously involved with one of the ID units in Fuller's simulator.

"What *did* happen to the drawing?"

"It was deprogramed."

"Right there on the spot?"

"Yes."

"Explain how it was done."

"We knew it was there. After the Operator arranged Dr. Fuller's death, I spent a week monitoring his deactivated memory drums for any hints he may have left behind about his 'discovery'. We—"

I broke in. "You must have seen then that he had passed the information on to Morton Lynch."

She only stared ahead. That had been a statement.

"Didn't you see then that he had passed the information on to Lynch?"

"Yes."

150

"Why didn't you simply yank Lynch right away?"

"Because it would have called for reorientation of many reactors."

"You had to reorient them anyway, when you finally decided to deprogram Lynch after all." I waited, eventually realizing I had merely made another statement. I rephrased the thought: "Why didn't you want to reorient this world to the alternate fact that Lynch had never existed?"

"Because it appeared he would keep silent on what Fuller had told him. We believed he would eventually convince himself he had only imagined Fuller's saying his world was—nothing."

I paused to regroup my thoughts. "You were telling me how Fuller's drawing had disappeared. Go on with your explanation."

"By monitoring his deactivated drums, we found out about the sketch. When I went to Reactions to pick up his personal effects, I was to look for other clues we might have missed. The Operator decided to yank the drawing at that particular time so we could check on the efficiency of the deletion modulator."

Again, I paced in front of her, satisfied that I was at last getting a full measure of truth. But I wanted to know everything. From what she told me I might learn whether there was anything I could do to escape the Operator's sadistic intent.

"If you are a real person up there, how can you maintain a projection of yourself down here?" That question had been prompted by the sudden realization that *I* couldn't stay *indefinitely* in *Fuller's* simulator on a direct surveillance circuit.

She answered mechanically, without a trace of emotion or interest. "Every night, instead of sleeping, I go back up there. During that part of the day when I can reasonably expect to be out of contact with reactors down here, I withdraw."

That was logical. Time on a projection couch was equivalent to time spent asleep. Thus, the biological necessity of rest was fully provided. And, while she was withdrawn from this world, she could be tending to other physical needs.

I faced her suddenly with the critical question. "How do you explain being in love with me?"

Without feeling, she said, "You're much like someone I once loved up there."

"Who?"

"The Operator."

Somehow I sensed the imminence of revelation. I remembered how, during the latter instances of empathic coupling with the Operator, I had gotten the odd impression of a certain indefinite similarity between us. That checked.

"Who is the Operator?"

"Douglas Hall."

I fell back incredulously. *"Me?"*

"No."

"But that's what you just said!"

Silence—in response to a nondemanding assertion.

"How can the Operator *be* me and *not* be me at the same time?"

"It's something like what Dr. Fuller did with Morton Lynch."

"I don't understand." Then, when I received no response, "Explain that."

"Fuller facetiously recreated Lynch as a character in his simulator. Douglas Hall recreated *himself* as a character in *his* simulator."

"You mean I'm exactly like the Operator?"

"To a point. The physical resemblance is perfect. But there's been a divergence of psychological traits. I can see now that the Hall up there is a megalomaniac."

"And that's why you stopped loving him?"

"No. I stopped long before then. He started changing years ago. I suspect now that he's been tormenting other reactors too. Torturing them, then deprograming them to conceal any evidence that might be stored in their memory circuits."

I paced to the window and stared out at the early morning sky. Somehow it didn't seem reasonable—a material person drawing warped gratification out of watching imaginary entities go through simulated anguish. But, then, all sadists thrived on *mental* appreciation of suffering. And, in a simulectronic setting, the subjective quality of programed torment was as valid as the mental reaction to actual torture would be in a physical world.

Beginning now to understand her attitude, her motives, her reactions, I turned back to Jinx. "When did you find out the Operator had programed his simulectronic equivalent into his machine?"

"When I started preparing for this projection assignment."

152

"Why do you suppose he did it?"

"I couldn't even guess at first. But now I know. It has to do with unconscious motivation. A sort of Dorian Gray effect. It was a masochistic expedient. But he probably didn't even realize that he was actually providing himself with an analog self against whom he could let off his guilt complex steam."

"How long have I been down here?"

"Ten years, with adequate retroprograming to give you a valid past before then."

"How old is the simulator itself?"

"Fifteen years."

I sank back into the chair, confused and weary. Scientists had spent centuries examining rocks, studying stars, digging up fossils, combing the surface of the moon, tying up in neat wrappings their perfectly logical theory that this world was five billion years old. And all the while they had been almost exactly that many years off the mark. It was ludicrous in a cosmic sense.

Outside, the first hint of dawn was beginning to spread itself in a thin crescent above the horizon. I could almost understand now how Jinx might love someone who wasn't real.

"You saw me for the first time in Fuller's office," I asked softly, "and realized that I was more the Douglas Hall you had fallen in love with than was the one up there?"

"I saw you many times before then, in preparing for the projection assignment. And each time I studied your mannerisms, heard you talk, tuned in on your thoughts, I knew that the Doug Hall I had lost up there to his simulator was now down here in the same simulator."

I went over and took her hand. She surrendered it passively.

"And now you want to stay here with me?" I asked, slightly ridiculing her decision.

"As long as I can. Until the end."

I had been about to order her to withdraw to her own world. But she had unwittingly reminded me that I hadn't yet asked her the most important question.

"Has the Operator decided what he's going to do about Fuller's simulator?"

"There isn't anything he can do. The situation's gotten out of hand.

Almost every reactor down here is willing to fight to protect Fuller's machine because they believe it will transform their world into a utopia."

"Then," I asked, appalled, "he's going to destroy it?"

"He has to. There's no other way. I found out that much the last time I withdrew."

Grimly, I asked, "How long do we have?"

"He's only been waiting to go through the formality of consulting his advisory board. He'll do that this morning. Then he'll cut the master switch."

⚝SEVENTEEN⚝

Day was climbing well into the sky now as I stood before the window, watching the city come to life. High overhead, a stream of Army vans drifted by, apparently carrying a change of guard for the Reactions building several blocks away.

How inconsequential everything seemed! How useless were all purpose and destiny! How naive and unsuspecting was every reactional unit out there!

This was Doomsday. But only I was aware of it.

One moment life would be flowing its normal course—people crowding the pedistrips, traffic moving unconcernedly. In the forest, trees would be growing and wild life moving peacefully among them. With abandon, the lake would be tossing itself in gentle ripples upon the rocky shore.

The next moment all illusion would be swept aside. The ceaseless surge of sustaining currents would come to abrupt rest in myriads of transducers, halt in midleap from cathode to anode, freeze in their breathless race across contact points on thousands of drums. In that instant, warm and convincing reality would be translated into the nothingness of neutralized circuits. A universe would be lost forever in one final, fatal moment of total simulectronic entropy.

I turned and faced Jinx. Still she hadn't moved. I went over and stared down at her—beautiful even in her trancelike immobility. She had tried to save me from the horrifying knowledge that the end of all creation was imminent. And she *had* loved me. Enough

155

to share my oblivion.

I bent down and bracketed her cheeks between my hands, feeling the smoothness of her face, the only slightly coarser brush of dark, silken hair against my fingers. Here, she was a projection of her physical self. She must be as beautiful up there. It was an elegance of features and form that mustn't be wasted in a spirit of self-sacrifice based on misdirected devotion.

Tilting her face up, I kissed her on the forehead, then on the lips. Had there been the merest suggestion of a response? I was apprehensive. That would mean her suppressed volition was again beginning to assert itself.

I couldn't take the chance of having that happen. I couldn't allow her to be trapped down here when the final moment of simulectronic existence ended. If she were, then that would be the end for her too, physically as well as for her projection in my world.

"Jinx."

"Yes?" Her eyelids flicked for the first time in hours.

"You'll withdraw now," I directed. "And you won't project again."

"I'll withdraw now and I won't project again."

I stepped back and waited.

After a moment, I repeated impatiently, "You'll withdraw—*now*."

She trembled and her image became indistinct, as though obscured by convection currents rising from a sun-scorched traffic lane.

But the illusion cleared and once more she appeared solid.

What if I *couldn't* make her go back? Desperately, I reached for her gun. Perhaps another spraying of her volitional center—

But I hesitated. "Jinx! Withdraw! I'm *ordering* it!"

Her face writhed into an expression of protest and pleading.

"No, Doug," she muttered weakly. "Don't make—"

"*Withdraw!*" I shouted.

Her image appeared to be blurred by convection currents once again. Then she was gone.

I returned the gun to my pocket and dropped helplessly onto the edge of the bed. What now? Was there anything I could do except wait? How did one go about opposing an adversary who was omnipotent, an all-powerful megalomaniac?

When would it come? Would I be left at peace until that moment, or would he find time to play cat and mouse with me? Was my end to coincide with general deprograming of—everything? Or did he have something special in mind for me in advance of universal obliteration? Something similar to what he had prepared for Avery Collingsworth?

Disregarding the subjective approach for the moment, I wondered whether there was anything that could be done down here to make him change his mind about destroying his simulectronic creation.

I started going back over the facts. The usefulness of his machine was irrevocably threatened. Fuller had perfected a simulator within a simulator, the inner one intended to discharge the same function as the outer one. They were both meant to sound out public opinion by soliciting responses from analog human beings, rather than from actual persons.

In achieving its purpose, though, Fuller's counterfeit machine would make it impossible for the greater simulator to operate. For when Reactions began supplying predictions for marketers and government and religious institutions and social workers and the like, the pollsters themselves would be squeezed out of the picture.

The solution was clear: Some way would have to be found to preserve the Association of Reaction Monitors so they would continue on as the greater simulator's means of stimulating response among the reactional units down here.

But how?

There wasn't an ID unit in existence, outside of the ARM organization, who wouldn't rally to the defense of Fuller's machine. That was because Siskin had promised them so much through it.

Oh, the Operator up there could have Fuller's simulator destroyed outright. Another thermite bomb. Or even a bolt of lightning. But that would solve nothing. For not only would there be a universal move to rebuild it immediately, but the reactional units would hold the monitors responsible and would take their wrath out against ARM.

Any way you sliced it, the Association of Reaction Monitors was doomed. As a result, an entire world, a whole counterfeit universe had to be scratched off the books so a fresh start could be made.

At the window again, I watched the huge, orange disc of the sun slip into the sky, forcing back the haze of dawn before it. It was a sun that would never reach the opposite horizon.

✳

Then I sensed that someone was in the room with me. It was no more than a subtle realization that there had been movement back there—an almost inaudible footfall.

Without betraying my awareness, I casually slipped my hand into my pocket. I drew the gun and spun around.

It was Jinx.

She glanced down at the laser weapon. "That wouldn't solve anything, Doug."

I paused with my finger on the firing stud. "Why not?"

"No matter how much you spray me, it won't do any good. You might take away my will power. But each time I withdraw, that frees me from volitional paralysis. I'll just keep coming back."

Frustrated, I pocketed the gun. Force wouldn't do it. I had to find some other way. An appeal to reason? Make her realize she mustn't be caught down here when it happened?

She came over. "Doug—I love you. You love me. I saw that much through empathy coupling. I don't need any other reason for being with you."

She put her hand on my shoulder, but I turned away. "If we were coupled now, you'd know I don't want you here."

"I can understand that, darling. I suppose I might even feel the same way. But, regardless, I'm *not* going back."

There was only determination in the set of her shoulders as she turned toward the window and stared out over the city.

"The Operator hasn't cut in on you, has he?" she asked.

"No." Then I saw what I would have to do if I wanted to get her out of this world—and *keep* her out—before universal deprograming took effect.

"You were right about his coupling technique," she said thoughtfully. "Normally the reactor doesn't even know he's being cut in on. But there's a way to make the experience as painful as you want it for the subject. All you have to do is put the modulator slightly out of phase."

She hadn't been bluffing when she'd said that no matter how many times I paralyzed her volitional center, she would continue returning. The solution, then, was to order her back *just before* the final moment—when there would be no time for her to return.

I could catch her off guard, stun her, spray her volitional center—now. That would reduce her to a submissive automaton, of course. But she would be in my pocket. Then I could sit back and bank on the chance that there would be some indication when total deprograming was imminent. Maybe the sun, or perhaps some other fundamental props, would start popping out of existence first. When that happened, I would merely direct her to withdraw and hope that it would be too late for reprojection.

But when I closed in on her with the laser gun in my hand, she must have seen my reflection in the window.

"Put that away, Doug," she said calmly. "It's empty."

I glanced down at the meter. The indicator was on zero.

"When you sent me up there I could have returned sooner," she explained. "But I took time to program the charge out of that gun." She dropped onto the couch, folding her legs beneath her.

Crestfallen, I paused by the window. Outside, the belts were becoming clogged with people. Most of them were pedistripping in the direction of Reactions, Inc. The public demonstration Siskin had arranged was like a four-star attraction.

I turned sharply. "But, Jinx—I'm nothing!"

She smiled. "So am I—now."

"But you're *real*. You have a whole physical life before you!"

She motioned me over to the couch. "How do we know that even the *realest* of realities wouldn't be subjective, in the final analysis? Nobody can prove his existence, can he?"

"Hang philosophy!" I plopped beside her. "I'm talking about something direct, meaningful. You have a body, a soul. I don't!"

Still smiling, she dug a fingernail into the back of my hand. "There. That ought to convince anyone he has a body."

I caught her arm and twisted her toward me. "For God's sake, Jinx!" I pleaded, realizing I was losing ground in my attempt to get her back to her own world. "This is serious!"

"No, Doug," she said pensively. "There's no assurance whatever, not even in my own physical existence, that material things are actually material, substantial.

"And as for a soul, who ever said the spirit of a person had to be associated, in degree, with something physical? If that were the case, then an amputee dwarf would have to have less of a soul than a thyroid giant—in anybody's world."

I only stared at her.

"Don't you see?" she went on earnestly. "Just because we're down here, we don't have to replace our concept of God with that of an omnipotent, megalomaniac Operator of an environmental simulator."

Beginning to understand, I nodded.

"It's the intellect that counts," she said with conviction. "And if there is an afterlife, it won't be denied reactors in *this* world any more than it would be held out of the reach of ID units in Fuller's simulator or real people in my own existence."

She leaned her cheek against my shoulder. "There's no hope that this world will be saved, Doug. But I don't mind. Not really. You see, I lost you up there. But I've found you down here. If our roles were reversed, you'd feel the same way and I'd understand."

I kissed her then, as though the very next moment would be the last one before universal deprograming.

Contentedly, she said, "If it appears that he's going to let this world drag on for a few more days, I *will* go back up there—but only to preset the modulator for surge voltage. Then I'll return. A few seconds later, the coupling between my projection down here and my physical self up there will be broken—completely. And I'll be an integral part of this simulectronic world."

I could say nothing. I had tried to convince her. But, instead, she had convinced me.

The sun climbed up even with the window and cast its warming rays across us.

"He hasn't—cut in again yet, has he?" she asked.

"No. Why?"

"I'm afraid, Doug. He might decide to have another session with you before he switches off the simulator."

I felt the quiver in her shoulders and put my arm about her.

"You'll let me know when you're being coupled?" she asked.

I nodded, but again I wanted to know why.

"Because it might just possibly have some effect on him when he learns that I'm down here—for good."

I considered the Douglas Hall in that upper existence. In a sense, he and I were merely different facets of the same person. The phrase "in his image" swam into my thoughts, but I avoided the false theological overtones. He was a person; I was a person. He enjoyed an infinite advantage over me, of course. But beyond that, all that separated us was a simulectronic barrier—a barrier that had perverted his perspective, warped his mind, fed him delusions of grandeur, and turned him into a megalomaniac.

He had tortured and murdered ruthlessly, manipulated reactional entities with brutal indifference. But, morally, was he guilty of *anything?* He *had* taken lives—Fuller's and Collingsworth's. But they had never really existed. Their only reality, their only sense of being, had been the subjective awareness he had imparted to them through the intricate circuitry of his simulator.

Then I clamped down on my submissive reasoning. I would be no apologist for the upper Hall. He *had* murdered—viciously. There had been no trace of compassion in his disposal of those analogs who had seen through the illusion of reality. And he had not slain mere reactional units. He had savagely killed human beings. For self-awareness is the only true measure of existence.

Cogito ergo sum, I reminded myself. I think, therefore I am.

That had to be it.

I rose and walked back to the window, stared outside at the crowded pedistrips. I could even see a portion of the Reactions building. The scene over there seemed to be generating its own electric excitement. Hundreds of anxious persons, impatient for Siskin's promised demonstration of his simulator, were jamming traffic lanes, stalling pedistrips by their sheer weight and number.

"Nothing from the Operator yet?" Jinx asked.

I shook my head without looking away from the growing crowd. It was the people—the reactors—themselves, I reflected, who had stymied the Operator. They had made their own destruction inevitable.

The press of public opinion was like a solid shield protecting Fuller's simulator, which would have to be permanently destroyed if this world was to continue in existence.

Somehow it was ironic. Siskin himself was responsible for the mass attitude. He had manipulated the people out there even more effectively, through psychological appeal, than the Operator could through simulectronic processes.

For in order to change that overwhelming bulwark of public opinion, the simulectronicists would have to reprogram almost *every* reactor. It was too enormous a job. It would be easier to wipe all circuits clean and start over.

Then I drew erect and turned toward Jinx, my mouth hanging open in sudden realization.

She gripped my arm. "Doug! Is it—*him?*"

"No. Jinx, I think I have a plan!"

"For what?"

"Maybe we can *save* this world!"

She sighed hopelessly. "There's nothing *we* can do down here."

"Maybe there *is*. It's a slim chance. But it's *something*. This world—the Operator's simulator—is beyond salvation because the people, the reactors, insist on having *their own* simulator at any cost. Right?"

She nodded. "He can't change their convictions and attitudes short of complete reprograming."

"*He* can't. But maybe *I* can! Those people out there are all for Siskin because they believe his simulator is going to transform their world.

"But suppose they learn what his real motives are. Suppose they find out he only wants to become their absolute ruler. That he and the party are conspiring against them. That he doesn't plan to use Simulacron-3 *at all* as a means of lighting the way to social progress!"

She frowned and I couldn't tell whether she was confused by my suggestion or whether she was preparing to offer an argument.

"Don't you see?" I went on. "They would destroy the simulator themselves! They would be so disillusioned that they would even turn on Siskin! They might bring about the end of the party too!"

Still, she showed no enthusiasm.

"They would create an atmosphere in which Fuller's simulator could never be reintroduced. It would be simple, then, for the Operator up there to reorient a few reactional units like Siskin and Heath and Whitney. He could rechannel their interests away from simulectronics altogether."

"But that wouldn't free you, Doug. Don't you see? Even if you *did* save this world, you'd only be giving the Operator an unlimited future to apply all the simulectronic torture he can—"

"We can't be concerned with what happens to *me!* There are thousands of people out there who don't even suspect what's about to happen to them!"

162

But I could understand her viewpoint. My sympathy for the reactional units must certainly run deeper than hers. I was one of them.

Soberly, she asked, "How are you going to orient them to the facts about Siskin? There *can't* be much time left."

"I'll just go out there and tell them. Maybe the Operator will see what's happening. Then he'll realize he doesn't have to destroy this creation after all."

She folded her arms and leaned against the wall, uninspired.

"You won't have a chance to tell them anything," she said. "Siskin has the whole police force looking for you. They'll spray you down the moment they see you!"

I seized her wrist and headed for the door.

But she pulled back, almost desperately. "Even if you succeed, darling—even if you *aren't* sprayed down and do convince everybody out there—they'll only look on you as part of Siskin's plot. They'll tear you apart!"

I drew her across the room. "Come on. I'll need you anyway."

✖ EIGHTEEN ✖

OUTSIDE, THE BELTS WERE PACKED with persons pedistripping in the direction of REIN as I mounted the low-speed conveyor and tugged Jinx aboard. Before we reached the end of the block we had crossed over to the medium-paced strip. There was no room for us on the express belt.

Up ahead, a rumble of cheering voices rose like a wave. It was punctuated by the staccato of applause. In the next minute, Siskin's private car soared powerfully from the landing island in front of Reactions and headed for Babel Central.

Eventually I recognized the inconsistency in the crowd about me: There were no reaction monitors. Their absence, I realized, signified that ARM had abandoned its function—and that, consequently, the upper world's simulator was left without its response-seeking system.

Jinx rode the belt silently beside me, her eyes trained straight ahead, her face severe in detachment from the things about us.

I, too, was preoccupied with distant thoughts—thoughts that reached beyond the constricted infinity of my existence. I tried to imagine what the Operator was doing. Since our worlds were on a time-equivalent basis, he would certainly be awake by now.

He might be meeting with his advisory council at this very minute. That he had not yet coupled himself with me indicated as much. I had no doubt, however, that he would eagerly forge his simulectronic bond between us as soon as the formality of that session was over. And that would signify the end was near.

Under the great weight of their burdens, the pedistrips had slowed to a snail's pace. To my right, riders were stepping without difficulty off the express belt and pouring into the clogged traffic lanes to continue converging on REIN, two blocks away.

Jinx gripped my hand more firmly. "Any sign of him?"

"Not yet. I suppose he's still with the council."

But even as I denied it, I realized that he *was* coupled empathically with me. I could sense his presence now, much more subtly than it had ever been before, however.

The coupling this time was not generating the piercing, mocking pain that it had on previous occasions. Somehow I knew that for once he was merely observing impassively. If he intended torment, he was delaying it for some reason.

I glanced to the left, bringing Jinx into my field of vision. And I could sense his tenseness on intercepting that visual impression. Then I knew he was boring into my recent experiences, filling himself in on what had happened.

There was no mistaking his amused reaction, his sadistic surprise on learning that Jinx had committed herself fatally to his simulectronic rack.

Puzzled, I wondered why he hadn't started torturing me yet, why he hadn't thrown the coupling modulator out of phase. Then the answer became clear: One of the most pernicious forms of torment is letting the victim know anguish is imminent but forestalling it.

In response to that thought, the psychic component of his malicious laughter came through with almost audible force. I saw I could waste no more time, not knowing how much I had left. And, from that new anxiety, he seemed to derive an increment of pleasure.

We left the pedistrip and pushed ahead on foot, shouldering through the mass of people.

Hall? I thought.

There was no answer. Then I remembered the coupling was a one-way arrangement.

Hall—I think I can save *this simulectronic complex for you.*

Not even a suggestion of amused reaction. Was he listening? But, of course, he must already know what I planned to do. He *must* have seen it in my background thoughts.

I'm going to make this crowd attack Siskin's machine. I don't care what happens to me.

How much delight was he drawing from the halting fear and humiliation I felt in addressing him directly, presumptuously?

I'm going to arrange it so that nobody will tolerate Siskin's simulator. They'll even destroy it. Which is exactly what you want. But that's not necessary. Believe me. For we can have both Siskin's machine and your reaction monitors down here. All we have to do is see that REIN is used only for research into sociological problems.

Still no indication he was considering, or even listening to what I was saying.

I think I can turn public opinion against Siskin. They'll take their anger out on Simulacron-3. I won't be able to stop that. But you can. It would be simple. A violent thunderstorm—just after I get them riled up—would scatter them.

In the meantime, you could reprogram a few reactors. Wipe Siskin out financially. Plant a move for public acquisition of his machine. They would see that it was used for nothing but research into human relations. The justification for reaction monitors in this world wouldn't be reduced a bit.

Was he toying with me? Was his continued silence intended only to add to my anxiety? Or was he preoccupied with anticipation of my being sighted by police, or with how the mob would handle me when I shattered their delusions?

I searched the sky for indication that he had ordered up the thunderstorm I had proposed. But there wasn't a cloud in sight.

We were now in the final block before Reactions. And the street was so congested that I could hardly lead Jinx through.

Ahead fluttered the gaudy banner Siskin had festooned across the front of his building:

—HISTORIC OCCASION—
PUBLIC DEMONSTRATION TODAY
(COURTESY OF HORACE P. SISKIN)
REIN WILL SOLVE ITS FIRST PROBLEM
IN HUMANISM

Of course it was a fraud. Heath hadn't had time to reprogram the simulator for a new function. Siskin would eventually give the people some kind of idealistic double talk—possibly in preparation for a new legislative assault on the reaction monitors—after he let them cool their heels for a few hours.

The crowd lurched forward, carrying us along. And I was thankful for Siskin's "demonstration." There were thousands on hand to hear what I would have to say.

Jinx turned tensely toward me. "Surely he must have established empathy by now!"

But I was directing my thoughts intensely at the Operator in a final, unabashed plea:

Hall—if you're considering what I'm saying, there are just a couple more things. Dorothy Ford deserves better than she's had. You can wipe the sordid stuff through reorientation. Whitney will do a better job of supervising sociological research than Heath. And—find some way to get Jinx out of this. I can't.

We had reached the final intersection and I felt like a man who had been praying. The uncertainty that followed my shameless petition was perhaps analogous to divine supplication in at least one respect: You don't expect an oral answer from God either.

Then I felt it—the growing vertigo, the impact of roaring sound that wasn't sound at all, the nausea, the lapping of unreal flames against all of my senses.

He had thrown the modulator out of phase. And, through welling torment, came the empathically transferred impression of his wild laughter.

He had heard me. But my abject submission had only delighted him into a frenzy of anticipation.

Then it occurred to me that perhaps he had never *wanted* to save his world. Maybe, all along, he had looked forward to reveling in the horror of thousands of reactors as they watched their universe crumble beneath them.

The knot of humanity in which we were trapped surged ahead, then flowed to the left. Like a current sweeping around a piling, it parted to course past a pedistrip transfer platform.

Hurled into the waist-high structure, I put my arm out to break Jinx's impact with the metal ledge. Nearby, two policemen were trying to restore some semblance of order.

Hoisting Jinx onto the platform, I stepped upon the broken, twisted edge of a severed pedistrip and climbed up beside her. Twice we were almost pushed off before we could work our way back to the control superstructure.

Then, standing in the V-shaped recess, I evaluated our position. With steel behind us and on either side, we were exposed only from the front as we overlooked the surging tide of humanity that stretched out to the Reactions building across the street.

I gripped Jinx's shoulder and turned her toward me. "I wouldn't want to do it this way. But there's no choice."

Drawing the gun from my pocket, I twisted her around in front of me like a shield and held her about the waist. Then I brandished the laser weapon and shouted above the din for attention.

A woman saw the gun and screamed, "Watch out! He's armed!" She sprang off the platform.

Three men followed, one shouting in midleap. "It's Hall! It's that guy Hall!"

In the next second the transfer platform was evacuated, except for Jinx and myself. We were left standing alone in the forward recess of the superstructure.

I lowered the empty gun and brought it around in front of me, aiming its intensifier at her side.

The nearer policeman fought through the press of bodies to the edge of the platform and drew his weapon.

"Don't try to stun us!" I warned. "If you spray me, my reflex will kill her!"

He lowered his weapon and looked uncertainly at the other officer who had finally arrived at his side.

"You're all wrong about protecting Siskin's simulator!" I shouted. "He isn't going to use it to improve the human race!"

There were general outbursts of catcalls and someone hooted, "Get him down from there!"

Four more policemen forced their way to the platform and began spreading out around it. But they could go only so far without being blocked off visually by the superstructure.

"I don't think it's going to work, Doug," Jinx said fearfully. "They won't listen."

After the derisive response had quieted, I went on, "You're

suckers—all of you! Siskin's using you like sheep! You're only protecting his simulator from the reaction monitors!"

I was drowned out in a chorus of "Lie! Lie!"

One of the officers tried to climb upon the platform. I pulled Jinx closer and thrust my gun more firmly against her ribs.

He dropped back and stared in frustration at his own weapon. It was choked down to fully concentrated, lethal intensity.

I started to address the people again, but I only stood there trembling as the Operator turned his coupling modulator further out of phase. Frantically, I fought the thunderous roaring, the searing heat that raged in my head.

"Doug, what is it?" Jinx demanded.

"Nothing."

"Is it the Operator?"

"No." It wasn't necessary that she know about the coupling.

I felt her tenseness drain off. It was almost as though she were disappointed that my torment hadn't started.

The crowd quieted and I hurled out more frantic words:

"Would I be risking my life to tell you this if it weren't true? Siskin only wants your sympathy so ARM can't fight him! His simulator won't help anybody but Siskin!"

The upper Hall's modulator slipped further out of resonance and the inner roaring was a ravening torture. It was relieved only by the reflected impression of his brutal laughter.

I glanced up. There wasn't the merest suggestion of a cloud. Either he actually *wanted* to destroy his simulectronic creation or he didn't think I could reorient his thousands of reactors.

"Siskin only wants to rule the country!" I shouted desperately. "He's conspiring with the party! *Against you!*"

Again I had to wait for the vocal rumbling to subside before I could go on:

"With the simulator calling the shots for his political strategy, he'll be elected to any office he wants!"

Some were listening now. But the great majority was again trying to shout me down.

A score of policemen had surrounded the platform. Several were working their way around the rear of the superstructure. One was shouting something into his transmitter. It wouldn't be long before an air car would show up. And I wouldn't be shielded from its occupants by Jinx.

Across the street, several persons were moving about on the Reactions building roof. I recognized two of them—Dorothy Ford and the new technical director, Marcus Heath.

Anxiously, I turned back to the mass below. "I know about Siskin's plans because I was part of the conspiracy! If you don't believe me now, you'll be proving you're the suckers Siskin thinks you are!"

On the roof Heath raised a voice amplifier to his lips. His frantic words boomed down:

"Don't listen to him! He's lying! He's only saying that because he was kicked out of the Establishment by Mr. Siskin and the party and—"

He stopped abruptly, evidently realizing what he had said. He could have covered his slip by continuing, "—and the party and Mr. Siskin have no connection whatsoever."

But he didn't. He panicked. And, by fleeing back into the building, he helped prove my point.

That alone might have been sufficient. But Dorothy came through too. She picked up the voice amplifier and spoke calmly into it:

"What Douglas Hall said is true. I'm Mr. Siskin's private secretary. I can prove every word of it."

I slumped with relief and watched the mob surge toward the building. But then I shouted in anguish as the Operator, obviously displeased with my success, dealt out the full throes of faulty coupling.

Jinx exclaimed, "He's tuned in!"

Distraught, I nodded.

Then the pencil-sharp beam of a laser gun speared into my shoulder from above. As I fell, I saw the policeman clinging to his perch atop the superstructure.

I reached out to push Jinx away, but my hand went through nothing. She was gone. She had finally withdrawn to her own world.

Her disappearance startled the cordon of police, but only momentarily. Then another laser beam lanced out, spearing my chest. A third sliced me across the abdomen. A fourth hewed away half my jaw.

Blood spewing from the wounds, I rolled over and plunged into an abyss.

✖

170

When awareness returned there was the feel of soft leather under my body, the pressure of something heavy, tight upon my head.

Befuddled, I lay motionless. There was no pain, no burning flow of blood from my many wounds. Whereas a moment earlier I had cringed before the vicious assault of nonresonant coupling forces, now there was only a peaceful stillness.

Then I realized I could feel no pain because *there were no wounds!*

Confounded, I opened my eyes and was instantly confronted with the effects of a strange room spread out all about me.

Although it was a room I had never seen before, I could recognize the simulectronic nature of the equipment that filled almost all available space.

I glanced down and saw that I lay on a couch much like the one I had used before while coupled with reactional units in Fuller's simulator. I reached up and removed the empathy helmet, then sat staring incomprehensively at it.

There was a couch next to mine. Its leather surface still bore the indentation of the person who had occupied it—for a long while, judging from the depth of the impression. On the floor nearby were the shattered remains of another headpiece that had evidently been dropped or hurled aside.

"Doug!"

I started at the suddenness of Jinx's voice.

"Lie still! Don't move!" she whispered desperately. "Put the helmet back on!"

She was off to my left, before the control panel of a large console. Rapidly, she began throwing switches, turning dials.

Responding to the urgency of her words, I dropped back on the couch and sank into my bewilderment.

I heard someone enter the room. Then a sober male voice asked:

"You're deprograming?"

"No," Jinx said. "We don't have to. Hall found a way to save it. We're just suspending operations until we can program in some basic modifications."

"That's fine!" the man exclaimed. "The council will be glad to hear this."

He came toward me. "And Hall?"

"He's resting. That last session was rough."

"Tell him I still think he ought to take that vacation before he activates the simulator again."

Withdrawing footsteps evidenced the man's departure.

And suddenly I was thinking of that day in my office when Phil Ashton had come barging in on me in the form of Chuck Whitney. Like Ashton, I too had somehow crossed the simulectronic barrier between worlds! But how?

The door closed and I looked up to see Jinx standing over me.

Her face burst into a grin as she knelt and removed my helmet. "Doug! You're *up here* now!"

I only stared densely at her.

"Don't you see?" she went on. "When I kept asking you if he had established contact, that was so I could time my return!"

"You withdrew," I said, groping. "And you came up here. You knew you'd find him coupled. And you stepped up the circuit he was using *to sudden, peak voltage!*"

She nodded. "It *had* to be done that way, darling. He was destroying an entire world, when he could have saved it."

"But why didn't you tell me what you were going to do?"

"How could I? If I had, *he* would have known too."

Still dazed, I rose. Incredulously, I felt my chest and abdomen, my jaw. It seemed almost impossible that there should be no injury. It was a moment before I could assume the diametric perspective. In swapping places with that other Hall, *he* had come into possession of the mortally wounded body barely in time to take a final breath!

Floundering across the room, I passed before the shining metal surface of one of the modulators and saw my reflection. Feature for feature, it was I—as I had always been. Jinx had not exaggerated when she had said the physical traits of Hall the Operator and Hall the analog were identical.

At the window, I stared down on an altogether familiar street scene—pedistrips, air cars cushioning along traffic lanes, landing islands, people dressed just as the reactors in my own world were. But why *should* anything be different? My analog city had to be a valid reflection of this one if it was to satisfy its purpose, didn't it?

Looking more closely, I saw there *was* a perceptible difference. More than a few persons were nonchalantly smoking cigarettes. Up here there was no Thirty-third Amendment. And it was clear that one of the simulectronic functions of my counterfeit world was to test out

172

the feasibility of a prohibition against tobacco.

I turned abruptly on Jinx. "But can we get away with this?"

She laughed. "Why not? You *are* Douglas Hall. He was going to take a two-month vacation. With the simulator out of operation, I'll be able to take a leave too. We'll just take it together."

Eagerly, she continued, "I'll familiarize you with *everything*—pictures of the personnel, the facts and features of our world, your personal background and mannerisms, our history, politics, customs. After a few weeks you'll know Hall's role perfectly."

It *would* come off! I could see that easily enough now. "What about—the world down there?"

She smiled. "We can patch it up like new. You know what reforms and modifications have to be made. Just before I deactivated it, I had Heath energize Reaction's repulsion screen. When you turn the simulator back on, you can take it from there."

"There'll be a violent hailstorm to scatter the mob before they can crash through the screen," I said, suddenly enthused. "Then I'll have a whole schedule of developments and reorientations to program in."

She led me over to the desk. "We can get started now. We'll draw up a list of instructions and leave it with the staff. They can be taking care of the preparatory work while we're away."

I settled down in Hall's chair, only then beginning to realize that I had actually risen up out of illusion into reality. It had been a jarring transition, but soon I would become accustomed to the idea. And eventually it would be almost as though I had always belonged to this material existence.

Jinx kissed me lightly on the cheek. "You'll like it up here, Doug, even though it doesn't have quite the quaint atmosphere of your own world. You see, Hall had a flair for the romantic when he programed the simulator. I thought he showed a lot of imagination in selecting such background prop names as Mediterranean, Riviera, Pacific, Himalayas."

She shrugged, as though apologizing for the comparative drabness of her world of absolute reality. "You'll also find that our moon is only a quarter of the size of yours. But I'm sure you'll get used to all the differences."

I caught her around the waist and drew her close. I, too, was sure I would.